A Familiar Tail

Accidental Familiar 5

By Belinda White

Belinda White

Chapter 1

Opie leaned down and kissed me. I opened one eye to look at him. That was a big deal this early in the morning. He knew that.

The view from that lone eyeball was enough to get the other one open for a better look. My man looked really fine in his brown deputy sheriff uniform. Of course, he looked really fine without it too. But that view was for me and me alone.

"Be safe today, okay?" It was a daily thing I said. Well, on the mornings when he was here. In a few weeks' time, I hoped that would be every single day. I could hardly wait for that darn lease on his old apartment to be up already.

He grinned down at me. "Always." Then he sobered a bit. "You too, you hear?"

I gave a short nod even as my eyelids closed again, and I snuggled back into a sleeping position. "You got it."

His soft footsteps crossed the room, and I listened until I heard his car start down the long drive. I was still planning to sleep a while longer. Like Destiny would let that happen.

"It's time to get up."

She didn't even get one eyeball. "It's not even six o'clock in the morning. Come get me at eight, and we'll talk."

"You have work to do. It's time to get up." She

wasn't giving up easily.

I pulled Opie's pillow over my free ear. Like that would help. Destiny's words were more of a mind thing than a hearing thing. "I thought you weren't supposed to talk to me unless it was really important."

Even with my eyes shut, I could tell I'd offended her. She marched her tiny body up my legs and sat heavily on my shoulder, pushing her head under the pillow and leaning her cold and slightly damp nose right into my ear.

I jerked upright and glared at her.

"This is important," she said, looking altogether too smug for a tiny calico cat. "So I'm well within our communication agreement. We need to know what's going on in my council. Now. Not later."

It was tempting to sprawl back out again and try to ignore her. But I knew that really wasn't an option. Once Destiny got on a roll, there wasn't any sleep to be had.

"Don't you have other ways to figure out what's going on?"

Destiny shook her head. "I'm assuming you mean the Goddess? And the answer is still, surprisingly enough, no. She doesn't. This is being shielded from even her. Which is part of the urgency in this matter. If it's being shielded, then it just can't be good. Not to mention the fact that it takes a massive amount of power to shield something from the Goddess."

Okay, so now she had my attention. She hadn't mentioned this before. "She really doesn't know any more than we do?"

Heaven help us, that wasn't much at all.

"She knows an infinite number of things that you do not. But, unfortunately, not when it comes to her current council members." She paused. "Well, except for Opal and Patricia. They are still free and open to her.

Two of thirteen isn't all that great of an average."

"Do you think the other eleven are working together on something?" I shivered. That would be so not good. We're talking highest level witches here. A massive amount of power indeed.

She hesitated. "No. She doesn't think the corruption has spread to all the others. Not yet, anyway. We need to find the root of the problem to stop that from happening though." Destiny glanced pointedly at my bedroom door. "Now would be a good time." Then she paused and looked me in the eyes. "After you feed me, of course."

Of course. Even Goddess kitties have their priorities. Getting fed would always rate number one on the list.

We made our way downstairs and to the kitchen. Having Opie here most nights helped me out a lot. It's taken more than a little getting used to, having a fully stocked kitchen with all the necessary appliances for day-to-day life. The thing is, cooking I can handle. Kind of, anyway. At least Opie hasn't complained about it too much. That's something, right?

But the aftermath of cooking? The cleanup is something else altogether. I hate that part with a passion. Opie, having been on his own for years, doesn't seem to mind it all that much. We were so made for each other.

Of course, that deal only applied to meals he was present for. It wouldn't be fair to expect him to clean up after my breakfast and lunches. So, for those, I used mostly paper plates and bowls. Yeah, I know it isn't very environmentally correct of me, but I'm still a work in progress. I'll get there. Eventually.

I poured some of the kitty kibble that she liked into her bowl and a little milk into her saucer. No paper for her. She demanded glass dishes. Luckily, it wasn't a big deal to rinse off the saucer on a daily basis. The bowl with the kibble was pretty much self-cleaning as she emptied it.

Destiny looked from the bowl to me. Okay, so maybe saying she liked the kibble was a bit of an exaggeration. But she'd eat it if I didn't cave, so I took that as a win. For the cost of the stuff, she should. This wasn't your basic cat food. No, not for a Goddess kitten. This was top of the line kibble, dang it. Technically, she was eating better than I was. Nutritionally speaking, anyway. I'm sure the sugar count in my morning cereal was far more than a fitness-conscious person would allow. Good thing fitness-conscious wasn't a good description of me.

I was just sitting down at the table with my bowl of sugary goodness when the front door opened and Ruby pranced in. I glanced up at her and almost spit out my mouthful of cereal.

"What in good heaven are you wearing?"

She grinned at me and did a full three hundred and sixty degree turn in front of me. "The very latest in bounty hunting gear. Do you like it?"

Like wasn't the word I would use to describe it at all. But I didn't really want to hurt her feelings either. We'd settled into a bit of a pattern, and she was handling far more of the share of bounty hunting duties than me and Arc combined. As it had turned out, negotiation wasn't the only thing Ruby excelled at. She was a crackerjack hunter too.

Well, with my help. I generally did the finding thing on my trusty computer, along with interviewing witnesses, etc. But when it came time to actually bring them in? Turns out, Ruby was our Ace in the hole.

She had her very own taser gun and handcuffs too. And yes, she'd traded in her old pink and padded pair for a more regulation set of cuffs. Those first few take ins had garnered more than a few chuckles at the police station. And a few date requests for Ruby too.

Now that I think about it, that was probably one of Arc's reasons for gifting her the regulation set. He didn't want the competition.

Not that I blamed him. Ruby was a smoking hot witch if ever there was one. Good thing for Arc that she'd set her sights on him. He won the love lottery there. Both of them, actually. My brother was a mighty fine catch himself.

I squinted up at her, but the view didn't change. She was still dressed in some cross between vampire slayer and nature survivalist.

All black, of course.

Her pants were thick black leggings topped by an overcoat of some versatile material with about a thousand pockets—most of which were bulging with what she must have felt were necessities of her new trade.

For footwear, she had chosen a pair of black-dyed suede calf boots. Okay, so the boots I liked.

She must have seen my admiration for them because her smile amped up. "They get even better. Check this out." Then she stamped her heel against the floor, and a sharp three-inch blade popped out of the toe of the boot.

"What the…? What on earth would you need that for?" I thought about all the under the table kicks Arc got during our meals together. My brother wasn't all that great at polite conversation. This upped the threat a great deal.

Ruby laughed. Having grown up with me, she knew right where my thoughts had gone. "Don't worry, I'd never use it on Arc." Then she did a fancy roundhouse kick that ended with her right foot high in the air. About the level of a tall man's throat. "But you have to admit, it has promise."

"Hmm, I don't think I do have to admit that, actually." I paused. "Would you actually stab someone in the throat? Seems kind of drastic for the people we go after. It's not a dead or alive kind of thing, you know."

She put her foot back down and stamped the heel again. The blade disappeared. "I believe in being prepared. There might come a time when tasers and magic aren't enough."

If she said so. I'd pit my magic against her blade any day of the week. But then my magic trumped hers these days by a vast range. Who was I to blame her for trying to even the playing field a little?

Her eyes finally landed on my bowl of cereal. "Got enough of that to share? I haven't had breakfast, and my cupboard is pretty much bare."

Yeah, so was mine. "Sounds like maybe the two of us need to go shopping and replenish our stock." Before all of us went hungry. "But for now, help yourself, just go easy on the milk. Destiny will probably want seconds on that."

Ruby nodded and even filled up Destiny's saucer again before pouring milk into her own bowl. We all knew the chain of command around here. Not that Destiny was about to ever let us forget it.

There was a quiet woof from behind Ruby. I stretched enough to be able to see Yorkie Doodle sitting on the floor on the other side of the table.

"I don't suppose you have any of that kibble to spare too?"

I glanced over at Destiny. I'd be willing to share it if she would.

She gave me a kitty cat nod, and I finished off my breakfast and stood to pour Yorkie a small bowl of kibble. It was nutritionally balanced for a cat, but I wasn't so sure it would be good on a tiny dog's stomach. I didn't want to take chances.

"Okay, so now a shopping trip is absolutely on the docket for today. You know our familiars count on us to feed and take care of them, right?"

Destiny gave a woof of her own. What can I say? My cat is anything but normal. When I looked down at her, she gave a pointed glance at her litter box in the corner.

Oh, yeah. I needed more litter. There was barely enough to cover the bottom of the box.

Ruby laughed. "Looks like that's something we can both improve on, huh?"

A change of conversational topics was about due. I looked at her get-up again.

"Do I take it Vincent came up with another case for us? Or are you just showing me your new setup?"

She lifted one shoulder. "Nothing from Vincent yet. Although, he does seem to be impressed with our record so far."

He should be. Come to find out, the three of us made a heck of a good team. Bad guy bounty jumpers didn't stand a chance with us on their trail. What we couldn't find by old-fashioned means, our magic pretty much took care of. But we saved that as a last resort. It was more interesting that way.

"You think maybe we need to contact some other bond agencies?" Vincent was the largest, but not the only one in Oak Hill. And we could always go further afield if we needed to.

"Maybe soon, yeah. But for now, Boswell has something for us." She grimaced. "Not up to Vincent's standard of information, but it's what's on the docket for now."

She handed me a small piece of folded paper from one of her many pockets. I glanced at it and then back up at her. She was right. Not Vincent's standards at all. Basically, all we had from Boswell was a name, Al

Bork, and his last known address.
Just like old times.
This could be interesting.

Chapter 2

We were just getting ready to walk out the door when a car pulled up out front. I needed to work on some kind of alert system for that kind of thing. A little advance warning could be useful sometimes.

"Do you know anyone who drives a green Cadillac?" Ruby asked.

"No one comes to mind. You?"

"Nope."

Our curiosity didn't have long to wait, however, as the car parked and not one but two council witches got out. I felt Ruby's eyes as she looked over at me. "You've been behaving yourself, haven't you?"

I swallowed but nodded. I was pretty sure I hadn't used an abundance of magical power in the last month. Nothing large enough to get on the council's radar.

"There's only two of them. That should mean something, right?" There was a lot of hope in my voice. If the council was coming for me, there would be at least a Trinity. If not two Trinities.

"I'd feel better if one of them wasn't Tabitha Greenfield."

Yeah, so would I. I couldn't think of a single reason she and Ginger Forest would be at my door. Not that the not knowing stopped it from happening.

Taking a deep breath, and forcing a smile that I totally didn't feel, I opened the door. That's when I noticed that Ginger was holding a long, thin package. All wrapped up and with a pretty bow.

I glanced from the package to Ginger's smiling face. Maybe this wouldn't be so bad, after all. "Good morning, Ginger, Tabitha." I gave each of them their very own smile and nod too. "To what do I owe this unexpected visit?"

Tabitha grunted. "I told Ginger we should have called ahead, but she insisted it was friendlier to just pop in."

That sounded like Ginger, all right. But I was still waiting for the answer.

"I was hoping to make it out here before this, but things have just been so crazy lately." Ginger held out the present. "I got you both a housewarming gift." She smiled at Ruby over my shoulder. "Don't worry dear, I didn't forget you. There's two in there. I was just running low on wrapping paper."

Ruby started bouncing on her heels. She never was much of a one to wait when it came to unwrapping gifts.

"Please come in." A little late, but better than never, right?

"Oh, we can't stay." Tabitha's voice sounded very certain about that. "This is just a drop and run, right Ginger?"

"Oh, now, Tabitha, I'm sure we could spare a few minutes, couldn't we?" She went to step through the doorway, but Tabitha's angry stare must have been burning on the back of her neck, because she hesitated, and then stopped.

Ginger gave an exaggerated sigh, then nodded. "Now that I think of it, perhaps Tabitha is right. I did promise her a very quick drop off. I do hope you like the gifts. Ta-ta!"

And just like that, they turned, walked back to the car, and left.

That was… odd. And since when did Ginger start hanging out with Tabitha?

Ruby looked at me and then the package. "Can I open it now?"

I shrugged. "No reason why not." Then I paused. "It couldn't be booby-trapped, could it?" It would be just like the council to do something underhanded like that.

Ruby laughed. "Now you're just being paranoid. It's a gift from Ginger, of all people. You know it's gonna be something great."

As council members go, Ginger was a peach. She was the easiest of all of them to relate to. I'd even go so far as to call her… nice. Not a word I'm sure I'd apply to any of the others. Even my aunt Opal. I could, however, think of a few other fitting words that would describe most of them.

Ginger, though, was the exception to the mold of the witches' council.

I handed the box to Ruby, and she practically danced to the table to open it. The bow and wrapping paper didn't last long. You should see her at Christmas time. She usually left the tree area looking like a hurricane had gone through.

Glancing over her shoulder, I found myself more than a little curious too. "So, what is it?"

Ruby opened the box with a flourish and pulled out one of the items. The scent of cinnamon immediately filled the air.

"Oh! How perfect!"

Ginger had gotten each of us a cinnamon broom to hang in our kitchens. The absolute perfect housewarming gift for a witch. She was the master of giving thoughtful presents.

Ruby went off to hang her broom in her kitchen, and I stared down at mine sitting there on the table. I could feel my eyes growing moist.

Here's the thing. There's always a thing, isn't there?

Our contract to buy the property—and homes—we were currently living in, was made with Kyle. Kyle was our resident ghost's half-brother and a true moron. So much so, that he had, in point of fact, killed Liz just to get his hands on her wealth.

Too bad for him, he hadn't known the three of us were witches when he sold the place to us on contract, and well, things kind of got spoiled for him. It was all a misunderstanding on his part, as Liz hadn't remembered a thing about him being involved in her death. That is, until he showed up at our place with gun in hand. Then the memory floodgates had opened, and it all poured out.

Now, Kyle was in prison, where he belonged. That part of things is all well and good. The other part isn't nearly as nice.

With it now being known that he killed Liz, his role as beneficiary of all her worldly property went right out the window. Including, of course, his right to sell us the place on contract. The whole shebang was now in the hands of Patricia Bluespring. As it turned out, Patricia happened to be Liz's cousin, and her next closest of kin.

And that's where it gets complicated. I know deep in my heart that this place was meant to go to Patricia. Liz had even said so herself, so there was absolutely no room for doubt there. The place should be hers.

The trouble is, we all loved it here, and we didn't want to lose it. My dad and his awesome team of lawyers were looking into the possible avenues left open to us, but at this point, it wasn't looking good.

All we could hope for was that Patricia would

change her mind about wanting the place and let us keep it. To that end, we'd set up an Escrow account and had been making our regular contracted monthly payments into it. At least she couldn't say we were in breach of contract. We had that covered.

For now, we were doing what we'd started out to do. Hunt for bounty payouts and save up for the balloon payment at the end of the year. If there still was one. If not, at the very least, we'd have enough money to buy a smaller place.

But it wouldn't be this one, and that fact made me infinitely sad. I'm glad we got justice for Liz, but it's too bad that it might cost us the homes of our dreams. Where else would we ever find a place so perfect for all of us?

To make things even more complicated, I think I have Opie on the brink of moving in. His nightly stays here have increased, and the lease on his apartment was coming up at the end of the month.

A kind of now or never kind of thing. Or, to be more accurate, a now or next year kind of thing. Personally, I was hoping for the now. I liked having him here. And I like to think he liked being here with me too. A girl can only hope.

The case from Boswell wouldn't pay out all that much—his never did—but it was one small drop in our proverbial bucket of cases. Either way things turned out, we'd need a bucket as full as we could get it.

Ruby was back in minutes, and we cleaned up the breakfast dishes in a flash. Easy-peasy, as they were plastic wear. I put my foot down and insisted that Ruby change clothes while I showered and dressed myself. She wasn't all that happy about it. Ruby was inordinately happy with her style of choice. Me? Not so much. I wasn't quite ready to be seen in public with the new and improved Ruby.

Not really sure when I would be, either.

We hit the grocery store at full speed, then made a quick stop off at the pet supply store for more kitty kibble and dog chow. I even bought an extra bag of each and an industrial-sized tub of litter for my pantry. I didn't want to run so close again. After all, I had a Goddess kitty to take care of. And, as she'd made herself the spokescat for the other familiars as well, it was kind of important that we kept up our end of the whole familiar bargain thing.

If not, you could be sure we'd start hearing about it soon. Destiny and the others had already championed some changes to the place. The first being doggy doors installed on both homes. Good thing I liked Yorkie and Baxter, because they spent a lot of time at my house conversing with Destiny. Made me wonder sometimes just what the three of them were talking about.

And, more importantly, how it would end up affecting me. I was sure I'd find out soon enough.

When we got back to the house, I dropped Ruby off at the barn with all her packages and then drove up the short driveway in between back to my home. The sight of it used to feel me with a sense of true home coming. Now that things were up in the air, that feeling was still there, but laced with a sense of dread that it would all be gone soon.

I didn't like that part of the feeling at all.

When I got in, the only familiar in residence was Destiny. But she didn't seem her usually happy self. She seemed worried.

"Is something wrong, Destiny?"

She tilted her tiny head, obviously thinking the question over thoroughly before finally shaking her head. "No, probably not. I just haven't heard from the Goddess in a couple of hours." She shook herself.

"Probably nothing. She's most likely just busy with other things."

I heard her words, or thoughts or whatever the heck they were, but I could see that she didn't believe them. Something was going on. And if Destiny didn't like it, I didn't like it. But there wasn't any sense in pestering her with questions that would only upset her further. Besides, these groceries weren't going to put themselves away.

"I see you bought two cases of that special beer that Opie likes. Is that a sign of good things?" she asked.

"Well, he has been staying here more than home lately. I kind of want to do my part to make sure that continues." Having his favorite beer in the fridge couldn't hurt that, now could it?

"Good. I like him. He's good for you. Keeps you grounded."

I'd have to take her word on that. The grounded part, I mean. I already knew he was good for me. We kind of were made for each other. Like Ruby and Arc. Good thing we'd all finally come together in one big happy family, huh?

Well, we were getting there at least.

Once I had everything put away, I started for the fridge to make myself a sandwich. Unfortunately, I found Destiny camped out in front of the door.

"Aren't you forgetting something?"

I thought about it. "No, I don't think so."

She rolled her eyes at me. I really didn't think most cats could do that. "The witches' council. Corruption. Ringing any bells yet? I let you slide this morning because... well, we needed food in the house, and I needed more litter in my pan." She gave a heavy glance at the still mostly empty box.

I took the hint and poured more litter into it. Not an easy task with such a large container. After I'd swept up the slight spillage, I looked at her.

"Better?"

She stepped daintily into the box and then gave me a look. Funny, but I didn't think most cats had a problem with privacy either. Lucky me to have such an original and one of a kind cat.

I glanced back at the now freed up door to the fridge. Destiny growled. That was all I needed to decide. Couldn't let my kitty get too cocky. Crossing over to the fridge, I pulled open the door and took out the makings of a sandwich. Bread, ham, cheese, and a little mayo later and I had a nice yummy lunch. Once I added a few potato chips to the plate, it was a full meal deal.

Only after I had my plate loaded down did I make my way up the stairs and into the office. That's where I found Liz. I'd been wondering where she'd been hiding.

Ever since finding out what had happened to her, she'd changed a bit. Knowing that you were murdered could do that to a person. Or a ghost.

She was still just as friendly, just not quite so exuberant. Part of that might be the fact that some of the newness of being able to communicate with people again had worn off. Another part might be the current status of who gets the house.

I could tell she was conflicted on that matter. No wonder. I mean, yeah, she'd always intended it to go to Patty. But on the other hand, if it hadn't been for the three of us, she'd still be stuck alone in a house with no one to talk to. And Kyle would still be free as a bird too. That had to mean something.

"Hey, Liz. Mind if I work in here for a bit?"

She looked up from the book she was reading. That was another perk of us living here. Before we came, there had been no way for her to turn the pages. But a little magic from the right witch can go a long way. And no, that right witch in this instance wasn't me. Or Arc or Ruby. It was Lily. She'd rigged a system to turn the pages that required only a slight temperature change. The one thing that Liz was very, very good at.

"Go for it," she answered. "Do you want me to go to my bedroom?"

I shook my head. "No need. I won't be making much noise, I promise."

She nodded. Then hesitated. "Can I ask you a question?"

From the somber tone of her voice, I kind of guessed what it was about. "Sure."

"If Patty cancels the contract and takes the property back, where will you all go? Back to your old homes?"

I took a deep breath. "I don't think that's possible. Not for me and Ruby, anyway. The old farmhouse is pretty much filled to the gills with Opal's new brood. Not much room for us there now." I paused. I didn't want her to think we would be totally out of options, though. Especially as it wasn't exactly her decision to make. I'm pretty sure the word of a ghost that no one but a witch could see or hear wouldn't go very far in a courtroom.

"Truthfully, it was time for us to move on, anyway. If we hadn't found this place, we'd have found another. And if Patty cancels the contract, then we get all our money back. Even the down payment. That, plus what we've saved so far, should give us the money we need to find some place." I glanced around. "It won't be nearly as nice as this, but we'll adjust if need be."

"I feel bad about that part of things, just so you know."

"I know. But you shouldn't. It's in Patty's hands now. Her decision." And I was pretty sure what the end decision would be. I was kind of surprised it had taken her this long to give us all walking papers. She loved this place too. I mean, what was there not to love?

It was perfect.

Chapter 3

I sat down and pulled the files on the witches I'd been given to check out in front of me. There were thirteen total witches on the council. Two of which had been given the all-clear by none other than the Goddess herself. Opal and Patricia Bluespring. The Goddess hadn't said we could bring the Minehearts into our investigation, so that left the work to me, Ruby, Opal, Mom, and Patricia. Five investigators and eleven possible suspects. Suspects to what, I still didn't have a clue. But if Destiny was right, the Goddess might not have a clue either.

That thought scared the dickens out of me. Who has the power to shield their lives from the Goddess? I wouldn't have thought that was even possible. If it was... well, wow. That was some kind of power. Power that had to be being helped along by one of the other not nearly so nice entities out there. There were more than a few of them.

I tried not to think of them much. Kind of pretending they were nothing more than scary tales to frighten children into behaving helped. At least until you got old enough to know they were very much real. Even if you couldn't see them, it didn't mean they weren't there. And watching.

Always watching.

A shiver crossed over me as I opened the first of my three folders. The others had voted to give me the odd one extra, as I didn't currently have a job. Now that Ruby had quit working at Opal's shop, technically she didn't have a full-time job either. But I was still the one with the extra file.

Not that it mattered much. This was something I enjoyed doing. Digging up dirt on powerful people. Who wouldn't like that, right?

The luck of the draw had given me Tabitha Greenfield, who happened to be second in command of the entire council, Gaston Crowe, and Constance Clearwater. Personally, my money was on Gaston, if for nothing more than his name. Gaston. The villain from Beauty and the Beast, one of my very favorite Disney animated movies of all time. By a wide margin too.

Unfortunately, because of that, I'd started my search with him and come up with absolutely nothing to show for it. The man was clean as a whistle. He was older, as most of the council were, but had lived an exemplary life helping the community at large. Not just the witch community either. Everyone. He had helped build houses for the homeless, worked in the area soup kitchen, and even rang the bell in a red Santa Suit at Christmas to raise money for charity. Granted, most of his charity work was to benefit the Native American community, but that was reasonable enough. The man was almost too good to be true.

Which would normally have me worried. But with all the balls he was juggling in his quest for possible Sainthood, I just didn't see him as having the time to cause trouble. Still didn't like his name, though.

As you might know by now, I really like the investigation part of things. I can really get into it. Which is why hearing the front door open what seemed to be just a short time after I started kind of startled me.

"Hi, honey, I'm home!"

Opie. And man, but did those words ever sound good. Maybe he was ready to announce that he was giving up the lease on his apartment and moving fully in here? Or just maybe I was reading too much into his television scripted line. I do that a lot.

I shut the files, stacked them back up, and closed my laptop. Then I went down to join my man in the living room. As I'd let time slip up on me and had absolutely nothing prepared for dinner, I was kind of hoping that he'd brought eats home with him. If not, tonight might be a fend for yourself kind of night. To be honest, sandwiches two meals in a row really didn't sound all that appealing.

Maybe I should get an alarm clock to let me know an hour before Opie was due home. Or better yet, just set the alarm on my phone. Yeah, I would totally do that tomorrow.

As I made my way down the stairs, I caught Opie sniffing the air. "No supper, huh?"

I could feel the heat creep into my cheeks. "Sorry. I did go grocery shopping today, so there's food in the kitchen. But I got tied up with work on the council thing, and spaced out for a few hours." He knew me well enough to know that was the Goddess' honest truth.

He drew me into a hug and kissed the top of my head. "Don't worry about it. I'll fix dinner tonight, and you can cover tomorrow night. And just for the record, I plan to call you before I leave work to remind you to put it on."

Hey, that would work too. "Deal." I paused, the guilt kicking in. "And I'll even help with supper tonight. How does my easy-peasy cheesy tuna casserole sound?"

Opie laughed. He knew that meant one of my signature single's only meals of macaroni and cheese with a can of tuna thrown in. Don't knock it until you've tried it. Might be super easy and quick to make, but it was still quite tasty.

"Did you happen to pick up any veggies on your shopping trip?" That wasn't the given it should be. I was more of a meat and potato kind of girl, and Opie had told me more than once that potatoes didn't actually count as a vegetable as they were more of a starch. Whatever the heck that meant. If it came out of a garden, to me it counted as a veggie.

"As a matter of fact, yes. I did." Thank you, Goddess, for reminding me! "There's a big bag of pre-made salad and two kinds of dressing."

"Please tell me one of those is Western?"

For that, he got my version of the Ravenswind look. I mean, come on, I knew him just as well as he knew me. What chance on the Goddess' green earth was there that I wouldn't have bought Western dressing?

"Let me guess," he said, after totally ignoring my look. "Western fat-free and Western regular?"

I nodded. Why buy something else that would just sit in the fridge forever?

After that, it was into the kitchen for a nice time cooking dinner together and then eating it. Once the cleanup was done, which took almost as much time as the actual meal preparation had, we stood at the kitchen counter and looked at each other.

"Want to take a short walk and get some air?"

I raised an eyebrow and gave a pointed glance out the window over the sink. January in Michigan meant not only frigid temperatures, it also meant it was pitch black outside very early in the evening.

"No, thank you."

"Okay then, how about inviting Arc and Ruby over for a board game?"

That sounded like fun. "Sure. You make the call, and I'll drag out the games."

But when I went into the living room, I found Destiny pacing back and forth in front of our makeshift game cabinet.

"Are you okay, Destiny?"

She hesitated in her pacing for the briefest of moments. Just long enough to give a quick shake of her head. "Something is wrong. Something is very, very wrong."

And that's when the wolf showed up at our door.

Chapter 4

An actual wolf. With fur and fangs and everything else along with it.

But that wasn't the worst part. The worst part was that Destiny was adamant that I let the darn thing in. Like that would happen.

I stared down at her. "It's bleeding. That means it's hurt. I don't think humans are good with hurt wolves. It'll bite."

"She won't bite. And she needs help." Destiny growled at me. Actually growled. "Let her in."

While I was standing there debating whether or not to go against what might or might not be a direct order from the Goddess herself, Liz flew through me. And no, I don't mean past me; I mean through me. Trust me, that's something you really don't want to experience if you don't have to. But I guess I was standing in the path to the door, and she didn't want to waste the extra Nano-second that going around me would have taken.

"What's going on?" Opie finally joined the party. He brushed past me, like a normal living person, and looked out our peephole, then back at me. "Why is there a bleeding wolf at our door?" His voice sounded a bit strange.

Most likely mine did too. "I don't know, but Destiny wants me to let her in."

His mouth opened and shut a couple of times before he finally got the words out. "I really don't think that would be a good idea."

"I agree. That's what I've been telling Destiny."

I looked out the peephole again. Liz was bending over the wolf, and for all the world, it looked like she was crying. Did she have a pet wolf we didn't know about?

Even as I watched, Liz's eyes rose to meet mine. "Please let her in. You have to help her."

The wolf, a beautiful gray creature for what that was worth, listed to the side and finally laid down on the porch, raising her own set of pleading eyeballs to the peephole.

Goddess help me, but I opened the door.

"Opie, would you please go upstairs and get a blanket out of the closet for her to lie on?"

"Like I'm leaving you with a hurt wolf. We'll use the throw from the couch, and I'll buy you another one."

I looked down at Liz and the wolf. "So, how do we do this? Can she walk in?"

Liz raised a ghostly and glowing tear-streaked face to me. "I don't think she can. She's barely hanging onto consciousness. Opie will need to carry her."

I glanced at Opie. "Liz says you need to carry her into the house." I don't blame him for the look he gave me. I'd have given that same look if someone had told me to pick up and carry an injured wild animal. But she was far too heavy for me to carry. I'm strong, but not that strong. He is.

He took a minute to retrieve the throw from the sofa and wrapped it around the wolf before lifting her as gently as he possibly could into his arms. That's my man. Doing what needed to be done, even at the risk of possible personal danger.

"Why is Opie holding a wolf?" Arc asked. Ah, yes, our company had arrived for game night. Too bad our fun plans for the evening had been canceled.

"We're still trying to figure that out ourselves," I told them. "But Destiny and Liz are both insisting that we bring her into the house and help her, so that's what we're doing."

Then something happened that changed everything. And I was very glad that Opie had wrapped the wolf in the blanket before picking her up.

Because when the wolf finally gave up and passed out, Opie was no longer holding a hurt and bleeding wolf. He was holding a hurt and bleeding Patricia Bluespring.

Any other man would have dropped her like a hot potato from the sheer shock. Not Opie, although he did stumble a bit. Then he carried her into the house and laid her out on the sofa. Only then did he look at me.

"Please tell me there's a spell that will change you into a wolf. I mean, Arc turned himself into a cat, right? This is a spell, right?"

I looked at him and then at Destiny. It was possible that it was a spell, but the timing was suspect to me. A properly performed spell wouldn't have just ended like that when she fainted. She'd still be a wolf.

But that truly only left one alternative answer. And it wasn't one that any of us wanted to consider.

Patricia Bluespring was a werewolf.

***

Which, of course, meant that werewolves actually existed. Something was telling me that was the big secret that the Goddess had warned us that Patricia would be sharing with us. The one she'd told us to be helpful and supportive of.

I had no problem being helpful and supportive, but man did I ever wish she'd told us her secret before showing up at our doorstep hurt and bleeding. We could have established some rules. Helpful rules.

"I'm calling 9-1-1," Ruby said, digging out her cellphone.

"No!" The voice from the sofa was little more than a whisper, but it was a very forceful whisper. "No ambulances and no hospitals. I've been shot, and there's more riding on this than just my life. I can't..." she paused, grimacing in pain. Then her watery eyes searched out mine. "Your mother... please..."

And then she was out again, and I was on the phone to Mom. Goddess help me, I didn't want to go into the whole werewolf thing over the phone, so all I told her was that Patricia had been shot and was at our house and refusing medical treatment from everyone but her.

Mom's only question... and I could tell she asked it while on her way out of the house already... was "It wasn't one of you that shot her, was it?"

I almost laughed. Stress sometimes causes me to laugh at things normal people might not find funny at all. "No. She showed up here after she'd been shot. I'd ask her who did it, but right now she's kind of going in and out of consciousness." I paused. "It looks like she's lost quite a bit of blood."

I heard the car starting in the background. "Being shot can do that to a person. Give us twenty minutes, dear." And then she ended the call.

Glancing down at Patricia, I made a decision. One I wasn't thrilled with, but twenty minutes is a long time for someone who is still leaking blood they can't afford to lose. Opie was already doing his part in putting pressure on the wound. Time for me to do mine.

It might not seem like it sometimes, but I do

listen to the Goddess and take her advice to heart most of the time. Anyone would be a fool not to. And I'm no fool. Well, not most of the time. So when the Goddess told me to start learning the art of healing from Mom, I had taken her at her word.

The trouble was, I wasn't very far along in my studies. But I did know one thing that might help in this situation.

Laying my hand over her heart, I let the magic flow into me. And then I concentrated as if it was my life that depended on it. This spell wasn't one to do lightly. It could end up causing more damage than good if I didn't get it right.

I sent myself into a trance to lower my own heartbeat and then, once my heart rate was pretty much bottomed out for a living person, I synched our hearts to beat in time. A lower heart rate meant much less force pumping the blood out through her wound. And that, added to the fact that Opie had found the injury and was applying pressure to it, just might be enough.

That was the hope anyway. It also helped that the wound was in her thigh versus her stomach. I've heard that stomach wounds are the worst. Too many things inside that a bullet can hit and do major damage to.

"I think the bullet went straight through," Opie said, looking closely at her leg. "That's good, I think." He looked up at me. "Your mom is really good at this stuff, isn't she?"

The unspoken question was the one that mattered here. He was asking if Mom could do as well as a doctor could for her. "Mom is the best. She can do stuff the regular medical people can't." I paused, drawing on some past memories of Mom doing just that. "She'll fix her up."

The only thing that was really worrying me was

the loss of blood. While it didn't look like an artery had been hit, her leg was covered in blood, and we had no idea how far she'd had to run to get to us. Or how long that had taken.

I was wishing she'd wake up already. Although, I know that was only being selfish of me. That wound had to hurt like heck, and she was better off if she could sleep through the pain. But a sleeping woman couldn't answer any of the million or so questions I had for her.

Chapter 5

It's a half-hour drive from Oak Hill, and thus from my Mom and Dad's house, to our new place. But it hadn't surprised me when she said they'd see us in twenty minutes. It didn't even surprise me when they made it in fifteen.

I'm just super glad that they didn't run into any police officers along the way. I'm pretty sure that telling them they were heading to a medical emergency when neither of them held any kind of medical license wouldn't hold much sway to the law. Then again, Dad probably had a spell to deal with that too. I know he had one to somehow increase the distance his car traveled in circumstances like this. That was one spell I didn't want to know how to cast. Too much trouble I could get myself into with that one.

That applied to any magic spell, really. But still. As a witch, I know my limits. And extreme speed in a car is one of them.

Mom went straight to Patricia when she got there, not saying a word. What was there to say?

Either Patricia had been playing possum on us, or her timing was extremely good, because just as Mom reached her side, she opened her eyes.

"The pain..." Her voice was weak, but Mom was already on it. She glanced back at me and Ruby. "Are the two of you willing to take on a little pain to ease Patricia off a bit while I do my work?"

My breath caught at the thought of it, but I nodded. Ruby did too.

Within seconds, pain flooded my body. I gasped, and Opie rushed to my side. "Can I take some of that?"

Mom didn't even look at him as she shook her head. "Sorry, dear, it's a witch thing." She threw the blanket off Patricia to see what she was dealing with. After a minute or two, her tensed shoulders relaxed.

That simple thing did wonders for me too. Not the pain part, but the stressed-out part was greatly relieved.

"I'll need some warm water, not hot, and a clean sheet to clean her up with." Mom smiled down at Patricia. "You got lucky. The bullet went straight through and didn't seem to hit anything major. You're going to be fine."

"Thank you. You work fast. I feel better already."

Well, yeah. That was because Ruby and I were shouldering about half her pain. It doesn't sound like all that much, but when you're talking about a gunshot wound, it is. A lot.

Mom glanced back at me. "You did the heart sync spell, didn't you?"

I nodded. "It was the only thing I could think of to slow the bleeding."

She nodded. "It worked. But you might want to release that spell now. I need to know exactly what I'm dealing with before I do anything."

No need to tell me twice. Having your heart synced to another was a weird experience all on its own, and with the added pain... well, I wasn't doing so great at the moment.

When the spell released, she gave me the

briefest of nods, then set to work with the supplies Opie had brought for her. We witches are used to naked bodies. Opie? Not so much.

Mom glanced at his bright red cheeks and took pity on him. "Why don't you go and get a clean blanket for Patricia, dear? And then maybe put this one in to soak?"

He nodded and hurried up the stairs.

"How long on this pain thing?" Ruby asked. It was a question I wanted an answer to as well.

"Not much longer, dears. I'd take it on myself, but I need all my brain power for this." She paused. "This will go a lot faster if I have a little extra juice, Amie."

I got the hint. "Take all you need, Mom." I'd told my family before that my magic was always at their disposal. They didn't have to ask. I trusted them to only use it whenever it was absolutely needed. And the whole using it for evil purposes wasn't really an issue. This was my family we were talking about.

We were the good guys here.

It was interesting to watch Mom work. I'd never seen her do anything quite this intense before. Healing sprains, bruises, even helping broken bones mend twice as fast as the doctors had predicted... all those things were old hat. Gunshots were new. At least they were to me. Mom seemed to take it all in stride a little better than I was comfortable with.

For all the world, it looked like this wasn't the first time she'd dealt with a shooting victim. That kind of had me worried. Was Mom leading a life I knew nothing about?

Then I glanced at Dad and knew the answer. Of course, she was. After all, I didn't find out who my Dad was until last year. Even then, it was kind of an accident. If you could call a grand Goddess plan an accident. She fully meant for the Ravenswinds and the Minehearts to be family.

Now we were. But I was starting to think that wasn't the only secret my mother was keeping from me. Not that now was the time to ask her about it. But soon.

I felt the magic flow from me to her, and Mom's hands started to glow. Even as we watched, the glowing hands touched Patricia's leg, front and back, and the magic ebbed out of Mom and into Patricia. The woman jerked and gasped as the magic hit her.

Unfortunately, Mom hadn't thought to warn us all of the added pain the magic would induce. Or maybe that had been her intention. Pull the band-aid off quick and without warning. Moms seem to think somehow that helps.

It doesn't. Not really. Pain is pain, whether you expect it or not. Ruby and I didn't.

We both went to our knees. Opie, who was just coming down the stairs at the time, took the remaining steps two at a time to rush over to me.

"Are you okay?"

I took a staggered breath and nodded. "Will be in a minute." My voice kind of squeaked. And I was really hoping my words were true ones.

Luckily, they were. The pain was intense, and I can't even imagine what it would have been like for Patricia had Ruby and I not been sharing the repercussions with her, but it only lasted a matter of a minute or so. Even if it seemed like much longer than that. Pain does that to the flow of time. Slows it down every single time.

But when the intensity flared and disappeared, it took a lot of the underlying pain along with it. I could breathe easy again. I took Opie's hand and got to my feet. "Just for the record, Mom, a little warning next time would be a really good thing."

She glanced at me with a sad smile. "Sorry, dear." Then she looked at Patricia, who appeared to have passed out again.

Maybe Ruby and I hadn't taken as much of a share of the pain as I thought we had. We were both up and going again. But then again, we hadn't just lived through being shot. Hope we never do, either. Although if we are shot, living through it would definitely be the option I would choose for either of us.

"I gave her a little relaxation spell, too, there at the end," Mom said, feeling Patricia's forehead. "She should rest easier now. We'll need to watch her for fever. If she pops one, we'll have no choice but to take her in to a hospital. Magic will only work so well against infection. Antibiotics are much better for things like that."

She leaned back against the couch and looked up at us. "Now, perhaps you'll all kindly tell me and Archie just what the heck is going on here?"

If only we could.

"Well, for starters, it looks like werewolves aren't fictional." I pointed at Patricia. "Either she's great at transformation spells, or she is one."

Funny, but Mom didn't seem at all shocked by that discovery. Oh, she tried to look surprised, but Mom is even a worse actress than I am. Somehow, someway, she knew about werewolves.

That didn't bother me so very much on one level. But on the level of she knew and didn't tell me, it bothered me a lot. She was getting a little too good at keeping secrets from me. And I really didn't care for it. I'd always thought we told each other everything. Then she ran off and married my dad, who I didn't even know until after the wedding. And now this?

What else was she hiding?

Mom must have seen that I saw through her

flimsy attempt at covering that little fact up. She looked me straight in the eyes. "Before you go getting upset and all angry at me, remember that this secret wasn't mine to tell."

"You knew about werewolves?" Ruby was a little late to the party, but she'd finally joined us.

Mom glanced up at the now sleeping Patricia and nodded. "I did. But only out of their need and necessity. A situation a bit like this one, actually."

"How long have you known?" Even I could hear the bitterness in my voice. Not her secret to tell? As long as she'd kept names out of it, I wasn't seeing the problem in telling her one and only daughter that werewolves were really a thing.

"Not all that long. About a year now, I guess. Archie and I were in Italy at the time. Then so much happened, and shortly after we got back to the states, there was that thing with Arc, and well... the timing just never seemed quite right to drop a bombshell like that."

Timing? She was blaming timing?

"Oh, I think you could have made the time for something like that."

"And exactly how would you have been better off knowing?" Dad asked, his tone strict. "It's not as if knowing about werewolves changes your life one single bit. They aren't the dangerous creatures that the old horror movies made them out to be. In fact, they're good guys like us."

"Persecuted by the regular humans like us too," Mom said softly, still watching Patricia. "They've had a much rougher go of it than us sometimes."

Rougher than Salem and the whole burning at the stake thing? I highly doubted it. But now wasn't the time to argue about that. Mom and I would be having a long talk later about all this. Now, we needed to figure out what had happened to Patricia and why.

I took a deep breath and pushed all the resentment and bitterness deep down. Well, as much as I could, anyway. "We really don't know anything. She just showed up at our door." I spared her a glare. "Not knowing about the whole werewolves are real thing, Opie and I were somewhat reluctant to let her in."

"What changed your mind?" Archie paused. "Let me guess, she passed out and changed back? They always go to human form when they sleep."

Good to know, but not exactly what happened. "Let's just say that Destiny and Liz were rather insistent that we helped her. She was actually in Opie's arms when she changed."

"Something I'm really hoping doesn't repeat itself," Opie said. "I almost dropped her." He paused. "I probably would have, if I'd known she was a werewolf. Too many of those movies in my past to see them as good guys, I'm afraid. I really thought she was just a witch. I mean, she is a witch, isn't she?"

"Yup, on the witches' council and everything." That was something to think about. "Does the council know?"

"Oh, heavens no!" Mom said. "And I don't think they'd be all that happy if they found out, either. That's part of the reason for the extreme secrecy." Her eyes locked onto mine. "I would think that you of all people would understand that."

Yeah, hold the whole Light Witch thing over me, Mom. Really cool. But she had a point. Maybe Patricia and I had more in common than I had previously thought.

Somehow that didn't fill me with warm and fuzzies like it should have. Having the threat of a Witches' Council sanction against you wasn't something you wanted to share.

Mom looked up at Liz. "Is there anything you

can tell us?"

Liz looked embarrassed but just shook her head. "Sorry, but not really. I am... well, was... a werewolf too. But we're Benandanti, and like you said, we're the good guys too."

Actually, as odd as it might sound, knowing that Liz was, or at least had been, a werewolf too, helped. I'd never really been all that fond of Patricia, due to the circumstances of our first meeting. But Liz I liked.

"Do you have any idea who might have shot her?" I asked.

Another head shake. "Being trapped here really limits me on keeping up with Patty. As far as I know, everything was going fine in her life. At least at the moment. But there's always the chance it was..." Her voice trailed off and her expression grimed.

"The chance it was who?" Dad asked.

Liz hesitated, biting her lip. "Well, I guess if you know about werewolves, you might as well know about our arch-enemies too. The Luparri."

All of us looked at each other. Nope. Not ringing any bells with any of us. But then we weren't werewolves.

"Who are the Luparri?" Mom asked. "And why are they your arch-enemies if werewolves are good?"

"Well, to be honest, only most of the werewolves are good. I mean, we're just like everyone else, we have our good and our bad. The good ones are the Benandanti. The bad ones are the Melandanti. You don't want to mess around with one of them. Trust me. The problem with the Luparri is that they don't see a difference between us. To them, all those who can change form at will are evil, and therefore must die."

"How many of these Melandanti are there?" Sorry, but right now that seemed important to me, even if I knew it was getting the conversation off track.

Liz looked at me with sad eyes. "Not that many. Again, we're just like regular people, you know. Not all of us are all that good, but very few of us are downright evil. You have to be pretty evil to be classed as Melandanti."

My shoulders relaxed. Okay, so that was good news. The last thing we needed was a sudden outbreak of werewolf attacks around town.

"I think we're getting away from the most important thing here," Opie said. His face was a little on the pale side right now, but he was soldiering through. Just like the sheriff's deputy he was. "Patricia has been shot. Werewolf or not, that's a major crime. We need to report this."

We all looked at each other, then at Opie. Uh-oh. This having a one hundred percent regular human in our midst might be a bit of a problem here.

Dad stood and put his arm around Opie's shoulder. "And just what would the report say? Someone shot a wolf, only it wasn't a wolf, it was a person?"

Opie looked conflicted. He believed in his job, and he was dang good at it. We were asking him to choose us over the proper law enforcement protocol. This could get dicey.

"Right now, we don't have enough information to report anything, now do we?" I asked, trying to help. "But I'm thinking the reason for reporting something to the law is so they can get to the bottom of what happened and see that any wrongdoer is brought to justice. Isn't that right?"

Opie knew where I was headed with this, but he gave me a reluctant nod all the same.

"Okay then. I'd say that, in just this one case, the proper authorities have been informed, and this will be investigated to the very fullest of our abilities." I smiled at him. "With our combined investigative powers and skills, that's saying something. We'll do her right, I promise."

"You sound like I've died or something," Patricia said groggily from the couch. "Am I hurt worse than I thought I was? Funny, but I'm feeling better now."

We all turned to her. Good. She was awake. Now maybe we could get some answers.

Chapter 6

When all the eyes turned toward her, she groaned. "Oh, Goddess, you all are going to grill me now, aren't you?"

Mom stood up and then looked down at her. "It seems to be a necessary step for us, you know. We need to know what we're dealing with. I take it you were a wolf when you were shot?"

Patricia nodded. "I was." Then she shut her mouth. Okay, this would take forever if our questioning was going to be met with one and two word answers.

"Look, Patricia. We get that you had to keep your little secret until it was absolutely essential for you to share it. Even though the Goddess told you months ago to come clean with us already. But that ship has sailed. No hard feelings." Well, that last part wasn't entirely true, but I was trying to keep the peace here. Set the tone and all that. "Now that we know about the Benandanti and all of that, it would be really helpful if you could tell us exactly what happened tonight. And please don't just say 'I was shot' and clam up."

She glared at me. "Telling you that I was shot pretty much sums it up in my mind."

"Okay, then if we have to do this the hard way, here are some questions we're going to need answers to. Do you know who shot you? Were you alone? Did the shooter know you were a werewolf, or did they just think they were shooting a wolf?" As horrible as that last part sounded, to me at least, it was a possibility. There were people out there that had an obsessive hatred of wolves.

She hesitated for far too long. I was just getting ready to let her have it when she held up a hand to stop me. "Obviously, I'm going to have to do some talking, but I'm really parched. Do you think I might get a bottle of water first?"

Personally, I thought she was just stalling to give herself more time to come up with whatever story she was going to give us. But Mom took pity on her and retrieved a cold bottle from my fridge.

I noticed a lot of glances between Patricia and Liz in the couple of minutes it took Mom to get the water. For all the world, it appeared to me like the two of them were carrying on a conversation. Kind of like Destiny and I could do. Mind talk without actually saying the words.

Could werewolves do that? And more importantly, could they only read the mind of each other, or other people (and witches) too? Suddenly I felt very uncomfortable around Patricia.

But I trusted Liz more. Looking over at her, I flat out asked it. "Can you guys mind talk to each other?"

She seemed taken aback, but she didn't outright deny it either. Instead, she looked at Patricia. So much for getting an answer from someone I actually trusted.

Patricia took a long sip of water before answering. Finally, she shrugged. "In a way, yes. It's something we Benandanti can do."

I must not have hidden my horror very well because she barked out a laugh. "Don't worry, we can't read minds, if that's what you're worried about. It only works between two Benandanti. And not nearly as well as we would like either." Her eyes were sad as she looked over at Liz. "And it's seriously hampered by only one of us being alive. I can barely get a read on Liz at all."

"Same here. I guess with both of us not fully in the mortal world, it messes things up."

"That's fascinating, dear, and something I'd like to hear about sometime in the future," Mom said. "But right now, we need to know about the shooting. The sooner we can get on that trail, the better."

Patricia nodded. "Okay, I get that. I'm afraid I'm not going to be much help, though. I really don't know all that much more than you do." She glanced at me and then back at Mom, obviously favoring Mom's style of questioning over mine. "To answer Amie's questions... I don't know who shot me. I wasn't alone, and I have no idea if the shooter knew I was anything more than a regular old, run of the mill wolf. If there is such a thing." She smiled. "Wolves are pretty special, if you ask me."

"Were you in a pack at the time?" Mom asked.

She glanced around the room before answering. "Yes, and no. My pack is kind of spread out over a few counties, but we try to get together every month or so. There's a park nearby that is kind of central to everyone. We meet there and take a run together."

"Lexie Park by chance?" I knew that park pretty well. In fact, I'd grown a tree there. A large one.

"I'd rather not give the name, if you don't mind."

"I'm afraid we do mind," Opie said. "Right now, I'm having a lot of issues with myself being in the same room with a gunshot victim and not calling in the local police force. Or at the very least, my dad. I've agreed to hold off and not report it as long as we investigate the incident fully between us. If that can't happen because you won't give us the details we need, then I'm making a call."

Patricia looked at him and then at me. "Is he serious? He'd do that? I mean, you're all asking me to divulge top secret information here. Information that could get me or one of my pack killed."

"Like what almost happened tonight?" Opie asked. "It's pretty obvious that Sapphire already knew about the whole werewolf thing, but I think it's safe to say that any secrets you reveal within this house will stay within its walls. And for the record, I'm very serious. Tell us and let us investigate, or I call in my dad and his crew. Your choice."

I couldn't have said it better myself. The ball was fully in Patricia's court now.

Finally, she blew out a breath. "Fine. It was Lexie Park, and there were five of us. One member couldn't make it as one of her children had a school performance that she didn't want to miss."

"When did the shooting happen? While you were all together?" We were more than okay with Opie taking over the questioning. Of all of us, he had the most experience in this kind of thing.

We weren't stupid. We knew that.

Another hesitation from Patricia. This was getting really out of hand really fast. I was beginning to be on Opie's side on the matter. If she would not cooperate with us, who she knew were good guys, then let her deal with the regular authorities. I was over all the hesitation to share her precious secrets with us. I mean, come on. After finding out she was a werewolf, what on earth could be so earthshakingly shocking?

"No. Thankfully, the others had just left the park. I stayed behind because I wanted to check out a tree there that's been puzzling me." Ruby and I exchanged worried glances. Although that park had lots and lots of trees, I was pretty sure I knew exactly which one puzzled her. And why. Full-grown oaks don't usually grow to maturity overnight.

And just like that, I realized that maybe I was being too hard on Patricia. After all, we had a secret we were keeping from her too.

"Maybe you'd better tell us exactly what happened in your own words. But I want everything that happened, understand? Anyone you saw, how long the others had been gone... everything."

When she still didn't say anything, he shook his head and pulled his cell phone out of his pocket.

"Wait. I agree to tell you everything I know. But I'm still not convinced it will help you. I just don't know much." She paused to take another few sips of the water. "We all got there around four-thirty or so, before it got dark. We had a short meeting in the back of one the others' van then changed for a quick run. As cold as it is out, even with fur coats, a long time of exposure to the weather just wasn't on the schedule. Not like our spring meetings. Those can go all night."

Another few sips. I could tell she was using the sipping time to gather her thoughts. As long as she followed her agreement to tell us everything, I was okay with that. The water would run out, eventually.

"After the run, we all said our wolfy goodbyes, and the others left. I stayed as a wolf. As I said, that tree had been bugging me for a while, and I wanted to check it out with my wolf's senses." She smiled again. "Nothing in this world will beat a wolf's sense of smell."

"How long had they been gone?" Opie asked again.

She thought for a minute. "Not long. I watched them all change, get into their cars, and drive off. Then I jogged over to the tree... it isn't all that far from the parking lot and started sniffing around the tree. That's when I was shot. The bullet tore through my leg, and luckily my brain kicked into high gear. I kind of figured that more bullets would follow, so I ran, three-legged style as far and as fast as I could."

"Were there more bullets?"

Patricia nodded. "One, but obviously it missed me. I didn't hear anyone following me through the woods, so I think they gave up and left. I have no way to know for sure. I was afraid to go back to my car, as they could have been waiting there for me. So I took stock of where I was and ran here."

"Lexie park is over five miles away. How did you make it?" I asked. Curiosity won out over the whole letting Opie be in charge thing.

She grimaced. "It wasn't easy, let me tell you. But with the way to the car... not to mention my clothes and cell phone... being blocked, it was the only thing I could think of to do."

Mom reached over and patted her hand. "And a good thing you did too. I'm not sure an injured wolf would have survived out there in the cold tonight."

Patricia's face was grim. "They wouldn't. Not without a den to go to. I'm going to be making a cache hole somewhere in that park from here out." Then she paused. "If we ever go to that park again. It might be time to change our meeting place."

"I'd say that would be for the best," Opie said. "But back to the shooting. Were there any other cars in the parking lot at the park? Did you see, hear, or smell anyone else at all?"

"No. And I mean no to all those questions. No cars, no sound other than the shots, and no people smell at all. Well, no current people smell." She and Liz shared another glance. "That's actually what has me worried. It might be the Luparri."

"Why would that make you think that?"

"Because the Luparri have the ability to hide their scent. Even from us, which is really saying something," Liz said. She looked at Patricia, her brow tight and her eyes flaring. "If it was them, then they know that you're a wolf. But it makes me wonder why they singled you out. Why not one of the others?"

Opie tapped his pen to his chin. When had he gotten a notebook and pen out? "I'm guessing they waited until one of the pack was alone. Unless Patty was their target all along." He put the notebook and pen away and shook his head again. "We just don't know enough to make that determination. One thing seems obvious, though. If it happened that close to the others leaving, the chances are whoever the shooter was, they may have seen them changing form. They could be in danger."

Patricia's eyes snapped to his. "My Goddess! I hadn't thought about that. If they didn't know who we were before, chances are they do now."

I nodded. "They could always run the plates on your cars too. Get their names and addresses, and everything else, that way." When she turned horror-filled eyes to me, I shrugged. "It's what I would do if I were a Luparri at a secret pack meeting."

"The question is, if the meeting was so secret, how did they find out about it?" Opie asked.

Yeah, that was the question all right. At least one of them.

Chapter 7

The first thing we had to do was check on the other pack members. Unfortunately, Patricia wasn't budging on the whole divulging their secret thing. I kind of understood. I mean, yeah, we totally had a reason for needing the information, but on the other hand, once we knew, we knew forever. Even after we found out if they were okay.

That made sense to me. But it still didn't help our situation.

Opie handed her his phone. "Call them and then erase the numbers from the phone."

She looked at him and then the phone. "How many phone numbers do you have memorized? That's what cell phones are for. They keep the numbers for you."

Okay, so she wasn't going to give us names, and she didn't have the numbers. Our next step was kind of obvious. Good thing the park was only a few miles away.

Opie and I volunteered to be the ones to go. Well, Opie volunteered, and I informed him that I was going too. Same thing in my mind. He wasn't all that happy about my company.

He was probably thinking the same thing that I was. Whoever shot Patricia might very well be waiting to see who came for the car.

Lucky for me, it was a fairly simple argument for me to win. After all, it seemed rather silly to just go to the park and collect the cell phone but leave the car. It made more sense to drive the car back here too.

And while Opie is great at a lot of things, driving two cars at the same time isn't one of them.

He wasn't happy about it, but in the end, he agreed. However, he did make one little change before we left. When we walked out our front door, he was in full sheriff deputy uniform. The hope was that if the shooter was still hanging around, which personally I doubted with the frigid temperatures outside, they would be given a start when they saw the uniform.

Something they wouldn't be expecting, given the circumstances of the situation. Werewolves wouldn't generally call in the police.

Of course, they might think that meant something else entirely too. Like maybe Patricia didn't make it, and her frozen and naked body had been discovered in the woods. According to Liz, if Patricia had died, her body would have changed immediately back to human.

A heck of a shock if someone had been just shooting from a sheer hatred of wolves.

Opie pulled into the small parking lot of the park, but the first thing he did wasn't head straight to Patricia's car. No, first he looked around and listened. Hard.

Nothing. The parking lot was pretty much surrounded on all sides by trees, so the line of vision from anyone sitting in a hidden car with a pair of high-powered binoculars would be extremely limited unless they were sitting out on the main road. And there weren't any cars there.

"Looks like whoever it was, hightailed it out

after the shooting."

Opie nodded. "Looks like. But be on your guard all the same."

We stepped out of the car and stood stock still for a minute. After all, we could always be wrong about the resolve of the would-be killer. It was possible they were still sitting high up in one of these trees with a rifle.

Not something we wanted to take a chance on.

When we finally made our way to her small Jeep, I casually reached under the tire well where the key was hidden in a tiny magnetic case. But Opie stopped me before I got into the car.

"I want to take a look at things first."

Ah yes, good idea. I waited as he took his ultra-high-powered flashlight and looked around the entire car and even under it.

"No sign of leaking fluid and everything seems to be untouched." But still, he hesitated. Finally, he held out his hand for the keys. "I'll drive this one back, just to be safe."

I stared at him. "Like I want to lose you any more than you want to lose me?"

He took a deep breath. "Remember that time your tire was shot out? If you had been driving instead of me, how would that have turned out? I've been trained in emergency driving situations. You haven't. Keys." His waiting hand made a small, impatient movement.

Well, if he was going to use logic, what choice did I have?

Only one that I could think of. Time. The car was covered in a very heavy frost. The kind that would require scraping and more than a few minutes of defrosting to be able to see out of the windows well enough to drive.

"You know, now that I think about it, it would

make more sense to leave the car here tonight and just grab the phone. I mean, we will be coming back to check things out in the daylight anyway, right?"

I wanted a better look around the park, but that would need to wait until morning. Yes, we were risking the crime scene being contaminated, but we didn't have the setup of a team of law officers. One high-powered flashlight wasn't enough to survey the area for clues and evidence. Not to mention possible bad guys sitting in trees with rifles.

Besides, this was a public park. People came and went on a frequent basis. It would be hard to determine if any evidence we might find would actually belong to the killer or some random, winter-loving jogger.

And also, it was cold. Very cold. Hopefully, that would work in our favor and keep the park visitors to a minimum until we could make it back for a fuller investigation.

Luckily, Opie saw the sense in my argument, and we left the car. Within fifteen minutes of leaving the house, we were back. Much faster than the trip would have taken an injured wolf. I was starting to have a pretty hefty respect for Patricia.

The last thing in the world she'd probably wanted to do was turn to me and my crew for help. And yet, she had. That meant she had brains.

That was a good thing. Especially since the Goddess seemed dead set on making her a part of our team. But then, maybe the Goddess had known this would happen and was merely preparing us for it?

Who knew? Certainly not me.

Opie handed her the phone we found in the glove box, and she immediately called the rest of her pack, one by one.

None of them were very happy to get the call. Not only because of the news that she'd been shot, but because they all had other lives to lead too, and they had been in bed asleep when the call came.

I'm guessing they really didn't like the ending of the call, when she told them they might be in danger too. If the shooter was from the Luparri, then chances were very good every last one of them was on his hit list now. A list complete with all the information he needed to find them.

If that was the case, then there was only one thing we could do to stop him. Find him first.

***

The next morning, Opie did something he very rarely did. He called in for work. Luckily for all of us, his boss was his dad, and he didn't ask too many questions.

Sheriff Taylor knew me and my family well, especially as it turned out, my Aunt Opal. So when Opie told him that he needed the day to help me with a particularly nasty investigation, the sheriff agreed to let him have the day.

"You realize I'll have to charge you a personal day, right?"

"Totally fine with that."

"Good. I can get a man to cover for you today, but tomorrow is Sunday, and I'll need you here. Things are tight on the weekends around here. And I have plans of my own, so I can't cover for you."

"I'll be there." Opie hesitated. "Even if I have to rope Arc into shadowing Amic tomorrow, I'll be there."

"Okay, then. See you then." And the call ended.

We bundled up as best we could and started to head out. Mom had stayed the night to watch over Patricia, and we'd brought down the mattress off the guest bed for her. We tried to sneak out past them without waking them, but it didn't work.

"Hold up there," Mom said. "I can take a wild guess at where you two are headed, especially seeing as how Opie isn't in uniform, but if you two will wait another few minutes, I'll fix you something to eat first."

Opie glanced outside, where the first rays of sun were just starting to appear. A few more minutes and it should be light enough for us to start looking around the park.

I waited, almost holding my breath. Yes, I wanted to get a jump on the investigation. But it had been ages since I'd had one of my mom's home-cooked breakfasts. I was kind of hoping that would win out.

Unfortunately, my man is made of sterner stuff than I am.

"Sorry, Sapphire," he said. "But I want to hit the park before any regular visitors show up. Plus, there is always the possibility that the shooter will come back after daylight to clean up things. I want to be there if that happens."

Even I admit his reasoning was sound. After all, this was a possible murder attempt we were talking about. Whether it was the attempted murder of an actual human or a wolf was the only real question. Either way, I wanted the person who did it to be held responsible.

Still, I wasn't giving up on the home-cooked breakfast quite that easily. Not now that the thought had been put firmly into my brain.

"If the offer would still stand a little later, we could call you when we're ready to head back." I couldn't keep the hope out of my voice.

Mom smiled at me. "That's a deal then." She paused. "You do have breakfast fixings, right?"

I nodded, suddenly very proud of my forethought in going grocery shopping the day before. "Yup. Use whatever you need."

We turned and just made it to the door when the knock came. It made me jump. Who the heck came calling at seven-thirty in the morning?

I opened the door to find out. Seconds later, I was laughing.

Before me stood Ruby in all her bounty hunting glory. I'd seen that before, but from the short cough-hidden laugh from Opie, he had not. That wasn't the source of my laughter though. No, she'd taken her outfit one step further.

She'd duplicated it for Yorkie Doodle. The tiny pup stood proudly at her feet, ready to go on the hunt too. And if that wasn't bad enough, Destiny was at her feet on the other side. In yet another matching outfit.

It was absolutely too much. Destiny took exception to my laughter.

"What? You think you're the only one who gets cold out here?"

"I hope you don't mind me dressing Destiny up too, but she looked interested in Yorkie's outfit, and I wanted to surprise you."

I grinned at her. Truthfully, I'd never in a million years have thought of putting clothes on Destiny. Up to this very moment, I'd have sworn she would have had nothing to do with that. Seems I was wrong on that count.

"If she's okay with it, I'm okay with it." I looked down at my familiar. "Looking good, Destiny."

She sat on her haunches. "Too little, too late. You laughed. When we're the only ones dressed for success here. Just look at yourself."

I glanced down at what I was wearing. For a cold morning out in the woods, I thought my old sweats were just about perfect.

"What's wrong with it?"

"Well, for one, that neon pink could be seen a

mile away," Ruby said. "You know, I have an extra outfit, if you'd like to change before we go."

Opie's slight cough changed to an outright one. "We?" He choked out.

She raised an eyebrow at him. "Yes, we. As in all of us, familiars included. Yorkie Doodle is a dog, you know. He's good at sniffing things out, so he'll come in handy."

Opie looked at Yorkie, who in turn wagged his tail proudly. I tried to hide my grin, but couldn't. I was perfectly fine with them tagging along. After all, the more eyes on the ground, the better, right? But it didn't take Sherlock Holmes to see that Opie had issues with the additional party members.

Or maybe it was just issues with being seen with them. Either way, he had issues. It isn't like he could do anything about them, but he had them.

We all piled in my little bug, with Destiny and Yorkie joining Ruby in the tiny backseat. Once we were settled in with Opie behind the wheel, she turned to me.

"That tree that Patricia was talking about..."

Opie's eyes snapped to the review mirror to look at her. "What about it?"

I swallowed and made a decision. We'd never really told Opie all that happened that night he came to our rescue after me accidentally growing an acorn into a mature oak tree.

"It's kind of a long story. Is it okay if I give you the Cliff Notes version?" He'd been with us on the magical side of things long enough to be able to handle the truth. I hoped.

"Sure."

"Remember that night I fainted in the park by that large oak tree, and you had to come help us?"

His face went blank, but he nodded.

"Well, we told you that I fainted when I used

magic for the first real time in my life. That was totally true, but there was a little more to the story. That tree hadn't been there when we got there."

The car swerved just the tiniest of bits as he took that news in. "That was a massive oak tree!"

I nodded. "Hence the fainting."

He was quiet for a minute. "And now Patricia is interested in the tree because..."

"Probably because she and her pack have been using the park for a while now. They had to have noticed that huge tree just showing up one day. Wolves would notice something like that, wouldn't they?"

Opie hesitated. "Being creatures of nature, I could definitely think that would be the case."

I shrugged. "So there you have it."

He glanced over at me, and then back at Ruby. "She really grew a whole bloody tree in a night?"

"More like a minute," Ruby said. "I came close to fainting myself."

Like that was saying anything. I'd been the one that had done it, not her. The fainting had come as much from shock as it had come from the sheer power that ran through me to do it. Not something I'd ever experienced before.

Sometimes being a Light Witch wasn't all fun and games. Like ever, really. Too much risk and not enough reward if you asked me. Not that the Goddess ever asked me. I still didn't understand how she'd chosen me.

By this time, we were pulling into the park, and our minds shifted to the here and now. We had work to do.

Chapter 8

We were kind of hoping to find the park totally empty when we got there, but unfortunately, that didn't turn out to be the case. When Opie pulled into the small parking lot, there was another car sitting next to Patricia's.

Not just any car, either. A sheriff's vehicle, and not one of Wind's Crossing. Most likely from the Oak Hill area. We hadn't had to deal with very many of them yet. I hated having to deal with law enforcement officers that I didn't know. It was all new territory to me.

The officer, a deputy by the look of him, was out of the vehicle and checking out Patricia's car. Opie stepped out and walked over to him.

"Is there a problem, officer?"

The deputy looked back at Opie. "Is this your vehicle?"

Opie shook his head. "No. It belongs to a friend of mine. She parked it here last night and then ended up going home with someone else. We're just here to pick it up." He glanced around the park. "And maybe to check out the park for a bit. It's kind of nice with nobody here."

The deputy smiled. "My favorite time to visit too. Although, I'll admit I'll likely prefer it in the other seasons. Winter was never my best time of year." He looked back at the car. "You might want to tell your friend that in the future it isn't a good idea to leave their vehicle in a public lot overnight without at least a note. If you hadn't got here when you did, I could have had it towed, you know."

"I know, and thank you for not rushing on that."

Opie was being a lot nicer than I would have been. Wasn't there some kind of time frame for you to collect your car from public property without it being towed? Then again, even if there was, would it be worth arguing with an unknown officer about it? Probably not. Maybe Opie was being smarter than I would have been too.

"No problem." The officer paused. "I'm fairly new to the area. Do you and your friend live close by?" He glanced over at our car, with me, Ruby, and the familiars still sitting inside and gave us a little wave. We shouldn't be able to cause trouble if we stayed put inside a vehicle. But after the wave, it felt a little rude, so us humans climbed out.

"We just moved in pretty close to the park, actually, but we haven't had the chance to make a lot of friends in the area yet either." Opie held his hand out. "I'm Deputy Trevor Taylor from Wind's Crossing."

The officer's eyes widened slightly as he took Opie's hand. "I'm honored to meet you. I've heard good things about your department."

Well, duh. Sheriff Taylor didn't run a sloppy ship.

Ruby and I stepped up, and Opie made the introductions. Well, our side of them anyway.

"I'm Deputy Steve Brighton, by the way." He paused. "I don't suppose you all would like to meet for coffee some time? Fill me in on the area a bit?" He smiled. "At least the Wind's Crossing side of it?"

Opie nodded. "Sounds good." He handed the officer one of his cards. Always prepared, that's Opie.

Such a boy scout.

The officer glanced at his watch and then gave us all a nod. "I've got to be going. Don't want to be late in my first week of work." But still, he didn't leave. "One more thing, though, did your friend happen to mention seeing any wolves out here last night?"

I almost swallowed my tongue. But Opie, Goddess love him, kept his cool.

"Not that she said, but as rural as it is out here, there is always that possibility, isn't there?"

He nodded slowly. "To see one or two, yes. But we had some reports of a full pack out here last night. I was just wondering if that was a normal thing for this area." He smiled at us. "I kind of fancy myself as a bit of a nature photographer. I'd love to get some good wolf shots. But I don't want to freeze my… heiny… off waiting for them if the reports were wrong."

I was suddenly very interested in tying my shoe. I just didn't trust myself to meet the man's eyes.

"I think I might wait for a bit warmer weather, if it was me. I'd like to see your pictures some time, though." Opie said.

"Sure thing. Maybe over that coffee we were talking about." He raised Opie's card in a kind of salute and then climbed in his car and buckled up.

We waited until he drove off, then looked at each other.

Ruby was the first to ask. "If you were driving by on your way to work, would you really be paying that much attention to see a car parked here? Is it even visible to the road?"

She had a point. The car was parked in the very back corner of the lot.

Opie glanced back at the road. "Maybe not, but he said he liked the park with no one around too. Could be coming here to gather his thoughts is his new routine." He shrugged. "Nature lovers that you witches are, you should be able to understand that." He hesitated. "Or maybe he was here checking out that report of wolves."

"That last one is kind of what I'm afraid of," Ruby said. "I'd feel better about it if he wasn't so new to the area."

He raised an eyebrow at her. "You thinking maybe he's a Luparii agent?"

She shrugged. "It would fit, wouldn't it? New to the area, good with guns, etc. Plus, he was here checking to see if the vehicle had been moved. That's something too."

Opie looked thoughtful, but didn't say anything. "Let's keep our minds open on that one, okay?"

Ruby nodded. "Sure."

I could so read between the lines of her one-word answer. We'd be investigating one Deputy Steve Brighton to the fullest. And as soon as possible. Ruby's observation made a whole lot of sense in the situation we were in.

With the deputy's car now gone, there were only two cars in the lot. Ours and Patricia's. Not that the absence of cars really meant anything. The park was within easy walking distance of a couple of housing additions. Early morning joggers would leave their house on the run, so to speak. They'd generally end up here for a loop through the trees at some point.

With the agreement to keep an open mind about Brighton, Opie's eyes went immediately to the big Oak. It kind of filled me with pride, actually. How many people ever got to see a tree they planted reach this kind of maturity? And I hadn't even planted the thing.

His eyes went from the tree, to me, and back to the tree without him saying a word. What was there to say?

"Did you want to take a look around the tree before I let the familiars have a crack at it?" Ruby asked.

Opie nodded. "Please. Keep them in the car for a bit longer."

I glanced in through the window. His words definitely didn't please Destiny, but then again, she was still sitting in a nice warm car. She'd get over it. It hadn't been my idea to bring her, anyway.

We walked over to the tree. When we were still several feet out, Opie stopped us. "Why don't you two give me a minute? Maybe you could look around and see if you can find where the shooter might have been waiting?"

Ruby nodded and started off. I waited until she out of earshot. "We'll be able to tell more where the shooter was when we figure out where she was shot."

He grinned at me. "Yes, but you can't blame a man for trying, now can you?" He paused. "But we do need to check out the area as quickly as possible, so splitting up still seems like a good idea to me."

There was that logic again, dang it.

"Okay, but if you find anything, give a shout, you hear me?"

He nodded. "Likewise." Then his attention was fully focused on the area in front of him. I kind of knew how Destiny felt now.

Ruby had gone to the right, so I went to the left. Patricia had told us that she'd been standing in front of the tree with the parking lot behind her when she'd been shot. That narrowed down where the shot could have come from by half, anyway.

I turned in a slow circle looking around. Nothing jumped out at me as my brain went through the motions of imagining the night before.

The parking lot would have had cars in it. There had been five of them, so possibly five cars. There was also the possibility that some of them had come together, so maybe less than five.

Cars would have given some cover to the shooter, but all but one of them had been driven off before it happened. How much cover did one smaller car give a person? Not much.

So probably not the parking lot, then. If the person had been standing in plain sight, Patricia would have seen him. Or her. I guess the Luparii could have female agents as well as male.

Killing was kind of an equal opportunity kind of career. I should know, I've dealt with killers of both genders. All in the last few months, too.

My life has really changed since I found out who and what I really was. As to whether it's a good change or a bad one? The verdict is still out on that one.

Taking a deep breath, I forced my focus to the task at hand. The parking lost itself wasn't paved. Just a bunch of gravel thrown down to kill the grass and give vehicles a place to sit without bogging down in the mud. We hadn't had much in the way of precipitation in the last few weeks, a fact I was very happy about considering the time of year, so it was rather dusty.

Not much to tell from that. Footprints don't show on gravel. Or grass, for that matter.

I took another full turn. Ruby had disappeared completely. I trusted if she'd gotten herself into trouble, she'd have called out. She had one side of the lot covered, so I'd concentrate on the other.

The trees on my side got my full attention next. Most of them were big, mature trees. Those didn't hold my focus for long. They could have been used as a shield, but the shooter would have been taking a risk of being seen.

I glanced up. If I was out to hide myself and take a shot at someone, I'd be up on one of those branches.

The foliage might be down, and with it most of the cover, but in the dark? It was still a great place to hide. Especially if you were wearing camouflage. I was betting they were.

Walking slowly, I made my circuit along the row of trees facing the lot. When I came to one with branches low enough for me to grab onto, I stopped and took a closer look. On the fourth tree, I found what I was looking for.

Well, I hadn't known what I was looking for before I found it, but still. It was definitely a clue. A footprint.

Not on the ground, but on the side of the tree. It was dusty, and had been smeared, but it was obvious as all get out that it was a footprint. The kind that might be left from someone, you know, climbing a tree.

I glanced up and over at the main tree only to find Opie staring straight in my direction. I waved him over, just as Ruby came jogging out of the trees.

"Nothing on my side. Did you guys find anything? Time to bring in Yorkie?"

Opie looked rather pained, but he stayed polite. "Not quite yet, Ruby." Then he looked at me. "What did you find?"

I could have given my brilliant reasoning and logic that led me to my discovery, but in the essence of saving time out in the cold, I simply pointed to the footprint. "I think someone climbed this tree recently."

Opie hunched down for a closer look. "I think you're right." Then his eyes went into the tree, and he nodded. "Good work. I think you've found where the shooter laid in wait."

Ruby didn't look happy. She wasn't upset that I'd found something, just that she hadn't. I'd probably feel the same if it had been reversed. But she'd been the one to choose the right side.

"Did you find anything?"

Opie nodded. "Oh yeah. I think I found where one of the bullets lodged in the tree. I'm going to dig it out now." He must have noticed Ruby's growing impatience to be a bigger part of this. "How's about you let the familiars out to do their business—away from the tree—while I dig out the bullet. Then we'll see just how good Yorkie's nose is."

She smiled. "Deal." She headed back to the car with a lighter step.

"You really think Yorkie will be any kind of help at all?"

He just looked at me. Yeah, that's what I thought too.

It only took him a matter of minutes to dig the bullet out of the tree. When he was done, I asked if he was sure he got it all.

The look he gave me said a lot. "Yeah, I'm pretty sure. Bullets kind of crumple up when they come into contact with something solid like a massive tree trunk. But they don't really shatter into pieces that I could have missed."

"Good. Then give me a minute." I felt the breeze on the back of my neck as my hair started to float. Reaching out, I touched the damaged spot on the trunk and let one of my mother's healing spells flow into it. The spot glowed for a few seconds, and when the glow disappeared, the trunk was whole again.

Opie reached out and touched it in wonder. "Wow. That was... wow."

The breeze didn't seem to pick up all that much, but the tree's branches moved, anyway. I think it was telling us thanks. To Opie for removing the harmful bullet and to me for healing her wound.

I smiled up at it. "You're welcome."

"Meow."

Glancing down, I saw that Destiny was sitting at my feet. She looked altogether too pleased with herself. Like it was her work or something. But then, on a much bigger scale, maybe it was at that.

"Are we ready for Yorkie to do his thing?" Ruby was bouncing on the balls of her feet.

Yorkie seemed excited too, but I'm not sure he knew why. More likely he was simply feeding off of Ruby's emotions.

"You bet," Opie said. He walked back a couple of steps and went down to his haunches, pointing to a spot on the ground.

There was blood there. Not a tremendous amount, but enough to see it for what it was. A person's life force.

At Ruby's direction, Yorkie walked up and sniffed the spot. Then he immediately sneezed. Some scent hound he would be.

Then he took off running.

We followed.

After several minutes jogging through the woods and getting our daily exercise in to boot, Opie called him off.

At least he tried. In the end, I think it was Destiny that got the job done. Yorkie came back to us with his head tilted and a questioning look in his eyes.

"Good job, boy," Opie said, pointing to the ground and yet another spot of blood. "You really are good at this." He did a better job than I ever could have keeping the surprise of that out of his voice.

Ruby puffed up. Like she was the one Opie was praising or something. "Then why did you stop him?"

"Well, for starters, it's blasted cold out here. And for enders, we aren't really tracking Patricia. We know where she went. If something important had happened along the way, she would have told us."

Ruby deflated. "So all this was for nothing?"

"No, not at all." Opie shook his head. "We came this way in a rush, but on the way back, we all need to spread out and look for any sign of someone chasing her. I'm really not expecting there to be any, but it's something we need to cross off the list."

We did just that. Spread out and made our way back to the lot and the car. Without seeing a darn thing that would show that the shooter had followed her into the woods.

"So we didn't really learn anything?" Ruby asked. She seemed more than a little disappointed.

All I could do was stare at her. "Are you kidding me? We learned a heck of a lot. We know where the shooter hid out, we found the bullet, and we're pretty sure he didn't follow her to finish her off. That's a whole lot of information."

She lifted a shoulder. "Yeah, but none of it tells us anything about who the would be assassin was. We're no closer to finding them."

"I wouldn't say that," Opie said, holding up the bullet in a small plastic bag. Just like him to be totally prepared with evidence bags at hand. That's my man, all right. "Not everyone would have used a silver bullet."

I took a closer look at the bag, just as a glint of the sun's rays hit it and bounced off the silver metal inside.

My eyes went from it to Ruby and finally to Opie. "We know what that means, don't we? Whoever took that shot knew exactly what they were firing at. A werewolf."

Opie nodded. "It's sounding more and more like that Luparii Patricia was talking about."

"Then why do you look so puzzled?" I asked. It was a fair question.

"Because if the Luparii are as skilled as they led

us to believe, then I really can't see them giving up the chase without making sure they had a kill."

Crapsnackles.

My man had a very good point.

Chapter 9

Patricia was all smiles when she saw the silver bullet. "Thank the Goddess. It's not the Luparii."

Personally, I didn't think that was all that good of news. She must have seen my look.

"You don't understand how terrifying the Luparii are to us were creatures. There isn't any way to know who they are. Or where they are, as they can cover their scent." That caused her a moment's hesitation. "Although, if they weren't Luparii, then why didn't I smell them?"

Mom shrugged. "Seems to me there are other ways of covering up one's scent. I can think of a few spells that would do the trick for one, and I know a fair few hunters out there that have their own secrets about doing just that."

Patricia didn't look so sure. "Maybe. But for sure, the Luparii don't use silver bullets, so we can cross them off our list. That's wonderful news, anyway."

Ruby and I shared a look. I still wasn't seeing the upside here. "But the bullet is silver."

She nodded. "Yes, and the Luparii know that it doesn't take a silver bullet to kill a werewolf. Any old regular bullet will work just as well. They wouldn't go to the expense of having these made up."

"But someone did." I was pushing my point

home. "It might not have been Luparii, and maybe that is the good news that you think it is. But the fact is that whoever took a shot at you last night knew they were shooting a werewolf. And chances are they were in that tree for a while. Why didn't they try to take all of you out? Wolves can't climb trees, and bullets can fly pretty dang fast."

Opie was looking at me with respect. "That's true. Maybe they knew exactly who they wanted to hit." He looked over to Patricia. "And that would be you."

"So the question is, who knows you're a werewolf?" Mom asked.

Now that Patricia knew where we were coming from, she wasn't looking quite as relieved, or as happy. "Until now, I'd have sworn that no one but the pack knew. Well, and the Benandanti organization. They know all the were-creatures."

They had their own organization? Fancy schmancy. Then I thought about it. We witches had our council. Made sense that the werewolves had their own kind of thing. But then something struck me. Patricia hadn't said werewolves, she'd said were-creatures. I had to know.

"We are just talking werewolves here, right? Or are there other things we should know about?"

Patricia glanced over at Liz, who shrugged in response. "I don't see the harm in telling them, do you?" Liz asked.

"I guess not," Patricia said. Then she looked back at me. "The Benandanti take many forms. Wolves, cats... I even heard that at one time there were were-butterflies, but I've never met any of them in my lifetime. Chances are something that fragile died out eons ago."

"So you're saying that you aren't really a werewolf? More like a shape-shifter?" Opie's voice squeaked just a little on those last two words. Funny how he seemed to be okay with a werewolf, but drew the line at shape-shifters. At least, it was funny to me. Personally, I didn't see much difference.

Not that it mattered, as Patricia and Liz were both shaking their heads. "No. A Benandanti only has two forms, a skin one—the human part — and a fur or feather one, the were-creature part. Each family of weres has its own lineage. Mine are wolves."

"So you can only turn into a wolf then?" He sounded like he really needed her to say those words.

She smiled at him. "Exactly. Wolf or human are my only choices. Both are hard-wired into my DNA."

He nodded slowly. "Okay, then."

"To get back to the matter at hand," I said, now that Opie was back on slightly more solid ground. "We need to know who your pack mates are. We need to talk with each of them. They might have seen or heard something, even if they don't think they did."

Her face shut down, just like I knew it would. "That's not going to happen."

I looked at Opie. Was he going to play the tough guy here? Pull out the bringing in the authority card again?

He stared back at me and gave an exaggerated sigh. "I know we need to talk to them, but obviously that isn't going to happen until we gain more trust of each other." His eyes went to Patricia. "I'll make up a list of questions and have you ask your mates. Would that work for now?"

Her shoulders dropped a bit as the tension flowed out of them. "That's doable. Thanks for understanding." She glanced at me. "Unlike some people."

I opened my mouth, but Opie elbowed me. I closed it again.

The discussion might have continued, but that's when Mom announced that breakfast was ready. Everyone has their own priorities.

Food is right at the top of my list.

***

We didn't feel right eating in the dining room when Patricia was sacked out on the sofa. She could get around small distances, but Mom didn't want her on her feet any more than absolutely necessary. Things like going to the bathroom come to mind.

I had a lap table that I used for work sometimes, and we helped her prop herself up and then Mom put her food on the small table. We all took our plates into the living room to join her.

A little bit of Lily must have rubbed off on Mom, because the instant one of us started talking about the problem at hand, she shut us down. Okay, so it was me. She shut me down.

"There's time to talk about all that after we eat, dear," she said. "Right now, we have other things to discuss. Like who will take care of Patricia while her leg heals."

I almost choked on the bite of bacon I'd just taken. The weird thing was, I wasn't the only one coughing. Patricia was too.

"I don't need taking care of," she said. "I can make it to the bathroom just fine all by myself. Give me a couple more hours, and I can head back home." She paused. "Thanks to you, of course. I know that wouldn't normally be the case."

Mom shook her head. "That's not how this works. Magic works only so well at healing wounds like yours. You have two decent sized holes in your leg, Patty. You need help." She smiled. "Don't worry, it's not a permanent thing. But I'd say a minimum of a week. And I'd much prefer it if that stretched out to two weeks."

"Two weeks?" That was me and Patricia speaking together.

"Yes, dears. We don't want the wound breaking open again, and that means you will need daily doses of magic to strengthen the... bonding agent, I guess you would call it... that is holding the holes closed. Within a couple of weeks, the healing should be far enough along for you to start—start slowly, mind you—being a bit more active."

I swallowed but felt a bit better. If Patricia was going to need daily doses of magic, then that meant that Mom would take her home with her. Didn't it? Of course, Mom's next words blew that out of the water.

"I'd take you home with me, dear, but my little shop will not run itself. I'm kind of a one-woman operation, you know. But I'll come by every night after I close to check on you."

I'd almost forgotten that Mom had started her own business. Good Morning Muffins. It was a tiny little hole in the wall shop way off the main square in Oak Hill. Truthfully, I was amazed that she'd gotten the proper permits for it. Food vendors generally had a rough time of that. But it hadn't been a problem for her. I think maybe Archie had something to do with that.

Surprisingly, for such a new and out of the way place, it was doing quite well for itself.

"Couldn't you close the shop for a few days?" I asked. Then I held my breath.

She just looked at me. "The shop has only been open for three weeks. I can't bloody well close it down now. Even if it would be only temporary. I'd lose the customer base I've built up." She puffed up a bit. "Besides, they need me. And my muffins."

Of course, they did. Mom's muffins weren't your average run-of-the-mill muffins. No, the name of her shop kind of said it all. Each and every one of the tasty delights came with its very own Good Morning Spell. Kind of a good luck spell on a timer. I'm guessing it was a very good spell from the word of mouth advertising and traffic her shop was getting.

I knew how much making a go of the business meant to Mom. It wasn't that they needed the money. The Minehearts had more money than they could spend in a lifetime. No, it was more about giving back to the community at large. And maybe more than a tiny bit about proving something to Opal.

Mom had grown up as the younger sister, always in Opal's shadow. Kind of like I had been with my cousin Ruby. Never quite as good as she was. My story had changed with the whole Light Witch revelation. Mom's revelation was still in the works. The shop just might be it.

But it had been worth a try. Looked like I would be stuck with the nursing duties for the next couple of weeks. Oh, joy.

The bigger worry to me was getting Patricia up and out again as soon as possible. I didn't want her to start feeling at home. Not that I'm that bad of a hostess, mind you.

I just didn't want her to realize just how perfect this house was and decide for once and for all to kick us all out and take it back.

Chapter 10

We spent the rest of the morning going over the answers that Patricia had gotten from her pack members. No one had seen or heard anything out of the ordinary. That didn't come as all that big of a shock to me. In fact, it was what I'd been expecting. If they had seen or heard something, then things might have ended very differently.

The one that concerned me the most was the one that didn't show up for the run. In my mind, right now she was our number one suspect, even if I couldn't get Patricia to agree with that. Just thinking about it, though, it was the logical first stop in our investigation. If only we knew who she was, of course.

All we knew at this point was that it was a woman with a daughter somewhere in the tri-county area. Didn't narrow things down very much at all.

Finally, I just laid it all on the table for her. "Look. If you won't tell us what we need to know, then you will need to do the investigation yourself. And a good job of it too. No blowing over it because you know the person and don't think she could possibly be the one. Trust me, she could be. People will surprise you time and again with just how much evil inside they can hide."

And then you have the ones that aren't evil. Those were the really scary ones. The ones that thought they had a good reason for doing what they did. Newsflash. There is never a good reason to outright murder someone.

Not that I haven't wanted to do just that at times in my life. Shoot, we all have at some point or another. But we don't because we're normal, decent people. Not everyone can say that. The trouble was, it was almost impossible to be one hundred percent sure you were dealing with one of the decent ones.

Patricia blew out a puff of air. "Fine. I'll call her, and some people I know, and make sure she really does have an alibi. Would that make you happy?"

"Happy? No. But it would mark one person off the suspect list. That would help."

While Patricia made her calls, the rest of us concentrated on coming up with theories of our own. According to Patricia, she couldn't think of anyone who would want to kill her. I wasn't so sure she was right on that count. After all, I knew the woman, and she could be very exasperating. If she didn't rub me the right way most of the time, I was pretty much betting she had the same effect on others.

But had she rubbed hard enough on anyone to make them want to shoot her? That was the question.

"You know," Opie said. "It really could be a case of the shooter just hitting the first one they caught alone. This might not even be about Patricia at all."

That might be true, but it wasn't what my witch's intuition was telling me. I firmly believed it was all about Patricia. It could still be Luparii in my opinion, too. In that case, maybe she was only the first of his targets. If any of the other wolves started having issues, we'd know for sure. That silver bullet didn't mark them off my list as firmly as it did for Patricia. Who said a Luparii couldn't be a purist of the old days?

"Well, it wasn't Brittany..." Patricia stopped as

soon as she said the name. "Crap. I didn't mean to say that. But it wasn't her all the same. She was at that recital at the time of the pack meeting. And it was about an hour's drive away. No way it was her."

"One crossed off the list and no one else on it at the moment," I said. "We're making progress, just not any closer to finding the culprit."

Not having any witnesses other than Patricia to interview was really holding me back. Investigations can be a tricky thing. Sometimes, even when an interview doesn't bring up any useful information, it leads to another question to ask. One that I didn't think of before. It was all cumulative.

I glanced over at Opie. "Where do we go from here?"

He took a deep breath. "Until we know better, I say we work under the assumption that Patricia was the target. Better safe than sorry." Opie glanced at Patricia. "You warned the other pack members, right?"

She nodded.

"Good. Looks like we're going to get to know each other a whole better in the next hour or two."

She grimaced. "It's not like I have much of a choice, is it?"

He grinned at her. "Nope, no choice at all."

"Meow."

It wasn't a quiet meow, either. Destiny was demanding our attention. When all of our eyes were on her, she looked up into my eyes, sending her message deep into my brain.

I swallowed. "Um, guys? I think the getting to know each other will have to wait for a bit. The Goddess wants a meeting."

"I don't suppose you have any meditation pillows around, dear? Getting up from the floor is harder than it used to be."

I gave her an almost panicked look. "That won't be necessary. She's coming to us this time."

"Wha..." The word didn't even get finished before the knock on the door.

Mom was the closest, so she answered and immediately went to one knee. As did we all. Well, except for Patricia and Opie. Patricia because she lying down, and Opie because... well, he wasn't a witch.

"Rise, my children, we have work to do. And not much time to do it."

She stepped in and looked around, giving the place a small smile and a nod of approval. "I like what you've done with the place. This is nice."

"Thank you, Goddess." I glanced at Patricia. "I just hope we get to keep it."

Patricia's lips thinned, but she didn't say a word. That wasn't a very good sign. Then again, it probably wasn't best to air our personal matters in front of the Goddess.

"Everything will work out as intended, child." The Goddess walked over to Patricia and looked down at her. "I'm sorry this happened to you, but I'm afraid this is only the beginning. Things will get much worse."

She turned to face all of us again. "For all of you, I fear. Being on my team is going to put you in danger. If any of you want out, just say the word."

Out? What was she saying?

"I truly think I can safely speak for all the Ravenswinds when I say that we will stay on your team, no matter what happens. We are at your service always, Goddess." Mom said it much better than I ever could have.

The Goddess nodded. "I was counting on that, but I felt I should make the offer. I don't like putting any of you into danger." She made a face. "It's more my job to keep you safe. This just doesn't feel right."

"You are there when we need you. Right now, if you need us, we're here," I said.

Ruby nodded, as did Patricia.

The Goddess smiled and looked over at Opie. The one non-witch in the entire room. "And what about you, son?"

He swallowed... twice... before answering. "I'm on the side of good versus evil. Unless I'm mistaken, that kind of puts me on your team."

A faint glow surrounded the Goddess. It was slight, but it was there. I rather think that meant that Opie's answer pleased her.

"So be it, then. Welcome to the team." She glanced down at Destiny and her smile...and the glow... brightened even more. "Team Destiny, I think we should call ourselves."

Sounded right to me, and from the puffing up Destiny was doing, I could tell she approved of the name. Then it hit me.

"That's why you came to us, isn't it? To be able to include Opie in our meeting?"

She nodded. "It seemed rather rude to leave him out, don't you think?" Then her smile dimmed. "But as I said, not much time for me to be here. So, to the basics." Her eyes went to Patricia on the couch. "Tell them. Everything. If they ask, give them the whole and complete answer to their question. Even regarding the pack. Is that understood?"

Patricia blanched and started to speak but then changed her mind. She closed her eyes and nodded.

"Good. One thing down. Now on to my second point of order. This happening is an awful state of occurrence and could not have come at a worse time. The rot in my council is growing stronger, and it needs to be dealt with."

She reached down and picked up Destiny, as if

gathering strength from her. "This is a pivotal time in history, and the future is hidden from me. But the evil forces are gathering, and one of them has managed to infiltrate my own bloody council. The ones I should be able to trust above all others. And they are hiding it from me."

Mom gulped. "Hiding it from you? Is that possible?"

The Goddess wasn't smiling now. "If you had asked me that two months ago, I would have said no. Unfortunately, these last few weeks have proved my assumption wrong. It is indeed possible. How? I haven't a clue. But powerful magic is involved, and I don't believe that the source is human. At least, not all of it."

Another gulp. This time, I think it came from pretty much all of us. "Satan?" I asked. There were a lot of bad players out there, but he was by far the worst.

The Goddess lifted a shoulder. "Could be. Or one of his upper minions. Or another entity entirely. I just can't tell." Her face could have been set in stone. "I'm working on finding out just who and what we're dealing with. They can't hide from me forever."

"How can we help, Goddess?" Mom asked.

"By continuing with the investigation of my council. As serious as this case is," she gestured toward Patricia. "Finding out what is going on with the council is even more so." She looked at each one of us, meeting our eyes for a few seconds before going on to the next. "We can't dally, not even for this. I don't know if that was the intention here or simply a happy coincidence for them, but we can't stop. Not now."

Opie looked at me bend then back to the Goddess. "How about I take over the investigation for Patricia and leave Amie and the others to tackle your issue?"

The beautiful smile and glow were back. Opie was definitely pleasing her greatly. "That would be ever so wonderful, son." Then her shining eyes met mine. "I'm glad your eyes were finally opened to this one, child. If I were mortal, I'd be after him myself."

Opie blushed. He wasn't much of a one to take admiration. Even if he did deserve it. My man wasn't only good on the inside. He was a hottie on the outside. Personally, I'm glad the Goddess wasn't a mortal woman. I'd hate to have to go toe to toe with her over him.

She raised her eyes toward the ceiling and nodded. Somehow, I don't think that nod was meant for any of us. Her next words kind of confirmed that.

"I have to go. I'm needed. I'll give you all what help and protection I can, but..."

"We understand, Goddess. Go and be well," Mom said.

The Goddess nodded and then... disappeared. I'd kind of expected her to use the door, but she didn't.

Then, just a split second later, another knock came.

I opened it to find her standing there. "One more thing, lest you all forget with all the goings on. You need to go and get Athena. Patricia will need her." She paused. "And fair warning, she really isn't very happy right now."

And then she was gone again.

I felt movement at my ankles and looked down at Destiny rubbing around them. It was enough to make me gulp. Destiny and Athena were sisters and had that same Goddess Cat thing going on. If I had missed feeding her dinner and breakfast and left her alone overnight?

Crapsnackles.

I was so hoping that I wasn't the one that would be sent to retrieve her.

Chapter 11

I didn't get that lucky. Somehow, I'd known I'd be the one elected to go and fetch Athena.

Destiny was sitting there, looking altogether too proud of herself. "Don't look so chipper, little Missy," I told her. "You're coming with me." That got her attention. She wasn't quite so chipper anymore. "Think about it... you can talk some kitty-cat sense into her. Much more than I could."

Besides, if nothing else, Destiny could serve as my decoy. Pretty obvious from her reaction to the news that she realized that too.

Opie laughed. "It isn't a death sentence, you know." He paused. "In fact, if we could make a quick stop at that park on the way, I'll even go with you."

I raised an eyebrow but wasn't going to risk actually saying anything. Why take a chance on him changing his mind?

Patricia handed me her house keys and gave me directions to her place. "All I ask is that you just go in, pick up Athena... her traveling crate is in the entryway closet... and come straight back. I don't want you going into my office. Is that understood?"

Opie and I looked at each other and then nodded. "Got it. Go in, get the cat, and leave. No dawdling and no poking about. I think I can handle that."

Mom didn't look so sure. "Maybe I should be the one to go after all..."

Part of me wanted to jump on the offer. The other, and unfortunately bigger, part of me was offended by her lack of trust in me. I kissed her on the cheek. "I got this Mom."

Opie grabbed our small tool kit out of the kitchen, and we headed out to the car. Once we were situated, I gave the small metal box a pointed glance. "What's with the tools?"

He shrugged. "I want to see if I can get a measurement on that footprint you found on that tree. Maybe it can tell us a bit more about who we're dealing with."

"A footprint?"

"Meow." Destiny put her two cents worth in from the back seat. Opie glanced at her through the rearview mirror.

She had insisted on coming without her carrier, so she was currently sitting back there with full range of the whole car if she wanted. But she had to know that this was on a trial basis. Usually for longer car rides like this, I insisted on the carrier. This time, I'd been distracted enough to give in.

"I know, and obviously you know, but let's cut her a little slack, okay? Amie's had a hard time the last twenty-four hours or so. She's got a lot on her mind. I'm sure if she took the time to think about, she'd realize that a footprint can give all kinds of information. Things like choice of footwear, size of shoe, gender of the wearer..."

I glared at him. "Gender? Really? I don't think a woman in heels is going to be climbing a tree, so good luck with that. Besides, you know my favorite pair of hiking boots is technically a man's pair of boots."

He grinned at me. "Oh, I hadn't forgotten. But not all that many men wear that small of a size." Okay, so he had a point there. "But I guess technically you're right. But it will tell us something about the size of our opponent. And that's something." He hesitated. "If I can get a good measure of it."

I glanced out my side window to hide my smile. "Maybe you should climb the tree too? There might be even better footprints once you get up into it."

I'd thought I was being kind of mean, but Opie took my words to heart. "You've got a point. That's a good idea, actually. Maybe the shooter left some other kind of evidence up there too." He shot me a proud glance. "Good thinking."

First time I could remember getting a compliment that made me feel guilty. "No problem." From Destiny's slight cough from the back seat, I knew that I didn't have her fooled at all. She was a pretty smart cookie of a cat. And besides, with that mind link thing, I was never sure just how much of my personality rubbed off on her. Sometimes it seemed like the answer was a lot.

He pulled into the park. We got luckier this time. No cop, and no one else, either. We had the place all to ourselves.

Opie grabbed the measuring tape from the box and ran over to the tree. I stayed in the car with Destiny. No need for both of us to freeze our patooties off, right?

As I watched, he circled the tree and then held the measuring tape up to it a few times. Then he glanced up the tree. I could only imagine he was trying to figure out the best way to climb it. That's when even more guilt set in.

I had a history with climbing trees. In my youth, and heck still to this day, I climbed trees on a regular basis gathering ingredients for Opal's shop. The only difference is that now, I can actually use what I gather for myself too. So, even more trees to climb in my future.

But watching Opie, I was thinking he didn't have that same experience with trees.

"You should go and help him, you know."

I glanced back at Destiny. "What are you, my conscience now?"

She raised a kitty eyebrow. "Well, someone's got to do the job."

"For your information, I was just getting ready to go... before you said anything."

"Of course, you were. I was just adding my opinion to yours." There was more than a little sarcasm in her mind voice.

Taking a deep breath and bracing myself for the cold, I opened the car door and stepped out. Then I walked over to Opie, who was still making his way around the tree, trying to come up with a plan of attack. I took the measuring tape and scaled that puppy in record time. The only thing that slowed me down in the slightest was trying to figure out where the killer had actually parked it.

It didn't take me all that long to find it. And, as luck would have it, the branch directly beneath the one they had sat on, had a fairly nice footprint. Much better than the one on the side of the tree.

"Hey, Opie," I called down to him. "You still have that notebook on you? And a pencil or pen?"

"Of course."

"Think you could toss them up to me?"

He took a minute to choose the best position to get them through the lower branches, but on the third try, we had success. I forced my cold fingers into action. Yes, I was wearing gloves, but they could only do so much in a Michigan winter.

I didn't take a lot of time with it, because as my fingers got colder, it would become increasingly harder to get out of the tree safely. Grip meant a lot when climbing in and out of trees and frozen fingers just didn't work as well as they should.

Once I had the rudimentary outline of the footprint and my awkward drawing of the marks on the sole, I called down to Opie again. I didn't want another broken arm. I'd only had one broken bone in my body in my life to date, and that had come from falling out of a tree.

"Watch me on the way down. If I lose my grip and fall, catch me, okay?"

He nodded. "You got it." Then he paused. "But try not to fall, just in case."

Yeah, like my plan was to fall into his waiting arms. Although, now that I thought about it, that didn't sound half bad. Body heat and all that.

Unfortunately, I had to do without the extra heat. I made it down with all my bones intact and without my man having to save me. Go me.

I handed Opie the notebook and pen as we made our way back to the car. He let out a low whistle, then reached out and ruffled my hair. I hated it when he did that. He knew that too, which made it even more frustrating.

"Good job, frog."

"Frog?" I paused. "Let me guess. That's from another one of your movies, isn't it?"

He grinned at me. "We'll watch it soon, and you can see the context. I think you'll be impressed. Besides, don't frogs climb trees too?" He paused. "Of course, you were probably more monkey-like than froglike..."

"Don't even. Just leave it at a one-time frog, and let's move on."

His lips twitched as he chuckled. "Anyway, good job. We can match this up to some different shoes and get a general size, and maybe even identify the make of the shoe from the sole markings. It's more than we had before you... climbed that tree."

I took his short pause for what it was. He'd been about to reference a monkey again, and I would have been obliged to hit him. Opie's told me in the past that I don't hit like a girl.

"Ouch! What was that for?"

"As if you don't know."

He waited until the car was between us, and we were ready to get in to answer. "Okay, but I should have been given credit for not actually saying it."

I gave him an evil smile. "And that's the only reason I pulled my punch." He rubbed his arm and looked at me doubtfully. Okay, so I hadn't pulled it by all that much.

"Yeah, thanks."

The good news was that we'd left the car running, so it was still nice and toasty warm inside. I took off my gloves and held my fingers up to the heating vent. The numbness slowly started receding. Frostbite averted once again. I'd gotten lucky getting out of that tree when I had though.

"You need a better pair of gloves. Those are practically worthless."

I looked down at my thin knit gloves and then to his nice, insulated leather ones and had to agree with him. "Trust me, it's on my list."

"Well, move it to the top. The temperatures are going to be brutally cold this week and they're even talking snow. A lot of it."

Great, just what we needed during an investigation. Normally, I didn't mind the snow. Especially now that I wasn't trying to hold down a full-time job working for someone who, you know, expected me to show up to work every single day, weather or no. But eventually, my investigation would have to go off the computer and into the real-life world. I'd been hoping for warmer weather before that happened.

But with the Goddess' urgent warning, I was thinking that wasn't going to be the case.

Patricia's home was about a half-hour away. Not in Wind's Crossing, but between it and the next town over. In the country, that means a lot. The next town over wasn't all that close.

He pulled in, and I did a double take. Then I looked down at the paper with the address and directions and back at the house.

"You're sure this is it?"

He nodded, as dumbfounded as I was, apparently. "That's the address number on the mailbox."

Destiny pushed between the two front seats and jumped into my lap, then raised her front paws onto the dash so she could stretch and see the house for herself. "And that's Athena there in the window. This is it, all right."

Opie and I looked at each other and then climbed out of the car. I noticed he left the car running again. There wasn't a reason not to. We were pretty far down a gravel road, and there wasn't another house in sight. Just the one in front of us.

"Funny, but I didn't picture Patricia as a lover of tiny homes," Opie said.

I had to swallow. Seeing the place made me realize that there was no way in heck we would ever convince Patricia not to take our new place. You could have fit her whole house in our front room and entryway.

Not that it wasn't cute as all get out. It was. She even had a tiny front porch on the log cabin, with a tiny little one-person swing and everything. That one-person swing made me sad. It was obvious that Patricia didn't have a lot of company out here. What a lonely life she must lead.

Not like my life. Mine was filled to the brim and overflowing with family and friends. Right then I vowed to make an extra effort to turn Patricia into a friend. Not because that's what the Goddess wanted, but because she needed to have people in her life. Live people, too, not just the ghost of a beloved cousin.

I handed Opie the keys, and he unlocked the door and pushed it open. We stepped in. At least it was warm and cozy.

The whole downstairs was open. In the back left corner was a small kitchenette that kind of reminded me of my old farmhouse apartment. Between the kitchen area and the living room area was a short counter with a single bar stool pushed up to it. The living area had a short love seat—the kind with overstuffed arms. I could picture myself sitting on it all stretched out with my back against one of the arms. I could almost picture Patricia doing the same.

Better than a recliner as it would also offer seating on the off chance she did have a visitor come by.

The whole other side of the cabin was pretty much her bedroom. A nice tall daybed and matching dresser at one end of the space, and an entertainment center with a smaller flat-screen television at the other end. There were two bookcases lining the wall between the two, and a rocking chair sitting in front of them.

That was it for the downstairs.

"I don't see an office," Opie said, his eyes going toward the ladder up to the loft. "It must be upstairs, right?"

I nodded. "That would be my guess. But as we aren't supposed to go there, I'd say that was off-limits."

He gave me a look. "You know she isn't going to tell us what we need to know, right?" His eyes went to the ladder again. "What if there was a list of pack mates up there? They might be in danger too, you know. If we knew who they were..."

"If we knew, then what? We're only two people, Opie. And the Goddess effectively pulled me off that investigation. So, it's really just you. You can't protect everyone, you know." I paused, my resolve to treat Patricia as a friend gaining strength. Friends didn't snoop on other friends. "I say we respect her wishes."

He nodded. "She might have some kind of booby trap spell, mightn't she?"

"Yup."

His brow cleared. "Got it."

We collected a very ticked off Athena, after a lot of explaining and help from Destiny, and we left.

Chapter 12

When we got back to the house, Opie carried in Athena and let her loose. She immediately ran over and jumped on Patricia.

"Oof. Easy there, Athena," she said. "And watch out for my leg, okay?"

The cat stared into her eyes for a long minute. Somehow, I could just imagine the mental conversation the two of them were having. Patricia's expression helped. I really didn't think she would win this one. Athena wasn't a happy cat right now.

I gave them a minute and then smacked my palm against my forehead. "We should have brought you some clothes and stuff. I'm sorry. I didn't even think of that."

Patricia broke eye contact with Athena, seeming more than a little relieved for the distraction. "That's okay. I keep an emergency bag in the back of my Jeep, so I'll at least have a change of clothes and hygiene supplies. We can get the rest later."

Opie took the hint and went out to get her bag. While he was gone, I caught Patricia looking at me very closely. Head to toe kind of gaze.

"No, I didn't trespass into your office. So whatever clues you're looking for, you aren't going to find." I paused as her eyes went to the door. "And no,

Opie didn't either. You told us not to, right? We listened."

"Thanks."

It might have just been me, but that word seemed awfully grudging to me. Like she hadn't been expecting to have to say it.

Opie came back in and put her bag beside the couch. Then he looked over at me. "I'm going to make a run into town and see if I can do some shoe matching. I'd ask you to come along, but I know how busy your schedule is with Goddess thing, so I won't."

I took a deep breath and nodded. As much as I wasn't a big shopper, I'd love an excuse to get back out of the house again. Especially one that didn't involve a ticked off pussy cat. But he was right, I had other priorities to focus on.

"You might want to pick up an extra pillow and blanket." I looked over at mom. "Just how mobile will she be for the next few days? Do we need to figure out bathing and restroom stuff?" I mean, she'd made it to the bathroom this morning, but it had been a slow go, and I was pretty sure Mom was feeding her strength and healing the whole time.

Patricia bristled. "I can take care of myself. I sure as heck don't need anyone to bathe me."

I gave her one of our signature looks. "Heaven forbid I would ever suggest such a thing. I was just wondering if we needed to pick up any supplies to make it easier for you to bathe downstairs. All the full bathrooms are upstairs."

Heat rose in her cheeks. "Oh. Then I'm sorry for snapping. I'd forgotten that." She glanced down at her leg and then over to Mom. "I'm not sure I'm quite up to stairs yet. What do you think?"

Mom shook her head. "Definitely not yet. Maybe in a few days. But not today or tomorrow for sure." She scrunched her nose while she gave it some thought. "We have an old antique washtub that's still in pretty good shape. It would take some work to get it filled up out here in the living room, so it wouldn't be a daily thing. But I think it would be doable once to get you cleaned up good from last night's grand adventure."

"We wouldn't have to worry about heating the water first, that will help. I can heat it up once it's in the tub," I said. The plan could work, but it would be a big pain getting the water from the faucet to the tub and then emptied back out again. I was glad that Mom had stressed the not daily thing. Once, sure. More than once, I just didn't see it happening.

"Okay then, I'll give Archie a call and have him bring it by on his way to pick me up after work." Normally, the law office wasn't open on Saturdays, but according to Dad, work had been piling up lately. Their stellar reputation didn't help that. Weekend hours were becoming more and more normal, according to Mom.

I don't think she was very happy about that, either. Especially when she'd decided to only have her shop open on weekdays so that their weekends could be spent together.

"So, is there anything else I need to get while I'm out?" He looked over at Patricia and smiled. "And special food requests?"

She considered for a minute. "That depends on which town you're going to. If you're heading into Wind's Crossing, I could really go for a Carny's pizza."

Huh. Maybe Patricia wasn't so bad after all.

Her words got a huge grin from Opie too. "Oh, I think that just cinched the deal for where I'm doing my shopping. Carny's okay for everyone else?"

Like that would be an issue for any of my family.

***

Once he left, Mom helped Patricia with another restroom break. A little longer one this time, as she took the time to brush her teeth and wash her face. She even ran a brush through her hair. She looked a bit more presentable when she came out. But then she looked a bit more exhausted too.

Patricia sat on the couch and looked over to me. I'd been waiting, not wanting to run out on Mom. But truthfully, my computer and research were calling me upstairs. The fact that Patricia hadn't been given the okay to climb stairs yet made it seem like a bit of a haven to me. Right now, I really needed some alone time.

I wasn't used to having this much company for this long.

"Thank you for taking care of me," she said, her eyes not quite meeting mine. "I know I'm not your most favorite of people, and for good reason with our history, but I just couldn't think of anywhere else to go."

"You did right to come here, and you know it. You had to know we wouldn't turn you away." I hesitated. "Well, not once we realized you were an actual human, that is. I'll admit I had my doubts about letting an injured wolf in my front door."

She gave me a crooked smile. "I think you'd have had doubts about letting a naked witch in your front door too. Unfortunately, those were my only two options."

I thought about Opie's shyness. He wasn't quite as forward thinking about the whole nudity thing as we witches were. "You probably chose right, then."

"Yeah, I thought so too. Your man seems a bit old-fashioned." She paused. "But nice, though. He's really nice. I like him."

As long as she didn't like him too much, that was a good thing.

"He's a keeper all right." I was running out of small talk. "So, I guess I should get upstairs and back on my computer, huh?"

"Wait a minute, dear," Mom said. "I've been thinking. It seems to me that it's a rather large coincidence that this should happen now. Right at the moment when we're investigating the council. What if it's related somehow?"

I could feel the horror in my eyes as I looked at her. It probably matched the horror that I saw reflected in Patricia's. "You think a witch might have shot Patricia?"

Patricia shook her head. "That wouldn't be the council way, would it? If one of them… well, us… wanted to get rid of me, I think magic would be the weapon of choice."

"Would it?" Mom asked. "First of all, magic can be traced you know. They would have to hide their magical signature somehow, and that's not as easy as you might think it would be. In fact, it's very, very hard to do. Especially with a big spell like what would probably be involved in killing someone. Plus, there's the whole rule of threes to think about."

What Mom was referring to was the Wicca Three-Fold Law, sometimes known as the Law of Return. The basics of the law was that whatever kind of energy you put into the world would come back on you three-fold. Not something to take lightly. It's why most witches can be trusted to do the right thing most of the time.

It's also one of the reasons the Goddess' current problem was so upsetting. Not to mention incredibly scary.

I blinked at her. "So, if you shoot someone the

rule doesn't apply?"

Mom lifted a shoulder. "I would think it would, yes, but some witches are of the belief that the law really only applies to their use of magic. Not a belief that I hold, but there you have it. People who want to do wrong will find a way to have it make sense to them."

Patricia wasn't looking all that happy. "They could have hired it done too. How much bad energy return would you get if all you did was give money to someone to do the bad thing for you?"

"Exactly, dear. There are ways some witches feel that they can use to circumvent the rule of three. Not that I agree with them, mind you. I think the Goddess is far smarter than they give her credit for."

"Meow." Okay, having the meows in stereo was definitely something I would have to get used to.

Mom smiled down at the cats. "Yes, dears, I'm sure that you are smarter than we give you credit for too."

"Dang straight," Destiny beamed to me. From Patricia's half-smile, I can only assume that the same message went to her from Athena as well.

Darned if I wasn't starting to realize that just maybe me and Patricia weren't so far different after all. We both had powerful secrets that we were keeping from the council. And we both had mind communicating Goddess kittens. Maybe, just maybe, we could bond over that.

If I ever got over my fear of being discovered as a Light Witch and all the ramifications that discovery could have on my way of life enough to actually tell her. Not bloody likely to happen anytime soon.

Dragging myself back into the present situation, I took a deep breath. "Okay, so who on the council did you keep to check out?"

Patricia looked worried. Really worried. "I

thought I owed it to Crystal to be the one to check her out personally. Not that I doubted any of your abilities at all, mind you." Yeah, yeah, sure. I wasn't totally buying that line, but if it made her feel better to say it, so be it. "And the only other one I kept was Ginger."

Mom and I looked at each other. Ginger was a sweetheart of a person. It would be hard to believe that she would be capable of anything nefarious. Crystal, on the other hand, was Crystal. The leader of the Witches' Council. A position that she didn't exactly gain by being nice. In fact, there were several of us that had significant worries about her being the final decision maker for our kind.

Crystal Waters? I could so totally see her being our bad guy. Or girl, as it were.

Patricia was chewing her lip. "There's no chance it's Ginger, is there?"

Another glance between me and Mom. Luckily, Mom was the one who answered. I'm not sure it would have meant as much coming from me.

"Well, you never know what anyone is capable of, now do you? We've all been fooled before, and I'm sure we will be again. Is she my top suspect? No. But that doesn't mean she's off the hook yet. But I'd say we need to double down on your two for a bit and see where that goes."

She had a point. Or maybe not.

"Okay, hear me out. Is it okay if I just think out loud for a bit?" I asked. They both nodded. "All right, here is what I'm thinking. The Goddess has kind of implied, if not outright said, that we aren't just dealing with mere mortals here, hasn't she?" Again, they nodded. "Well, what if this was just a ploy to throw us off the scent? Make us take a trail that leads us absolutely nowhere to gain them more time?"

"Do you think that's how they knew I was a

werewolf? The other entity told them?"

I had to think about it for a minute, but finally I shook my head. "I don't think so. The Goddess has told us she's limited as to what she can tell us because if she lets us in on secrets we aren't supposed to know, it opens doors to the others. She hasn't done that, so I would have to assume those doors are still shut. Right?"

Patricia nodded slowly. "But no one on the council knows what I am." The color returned to her cheeks again. "The council doesn't like different."

Tell me about it. Try being a Light Witch.

Of course, I wasn't quite ready to tell her that.

Chapter 13

By the time Opie made it home, we were no closer to figuring anything out. Not that any of us had actually thought we'd wrap things up that quickly. It would have been nice, though, if we could have come up with a single clue.

He found me up in Liz's office. Yes, our bedroom had a small desk and chair, but Opie was the main one that used that. As long as Liz was kind enough to share her office, I was planning to use it. Being surrounded by books kind of helped get me in the mood to work. Who knew that would be the case? Before moving here, I'd have thought having all that reading material just feet away from me would be a huge distraction. Come to find out, they were… soothing to the soul. Even the soul that was currently working.

Bending down, he kissed the top of my head and then took a quick glance at the screen. I felt rather than saw his double take.

"What the heck are you watching?" A slight pause. "Pornography? Really?"

It would have to be watered down quite a bit, in my opinion, to be classified as simple pornography. No, what I was watching was nasty to the extreme.

"I wish. This, believe it or not, is research. The other side of witchcraft. I'm watching some of these black market witch videos I found online to see if maybe I can find someone I know."

He took another look at the screen, even though I could tell from the tension in his body that he really didn't want to.

"Aren't most of them wearing masks and hoods?"

"Yup. But they don't wear them all the time. Some of the other videos show their faces."

"Then why are you watching this one? If you can't identify them, why put yourself through the pain?" He hesitated a little too long. "You aren't enjoying this, are you?"

"Goddess, no! But I have to watch it because, even with their faces covered, some of the more… interesting… participants have distinguishing marks." I tapped the notebook beside my keyboard. "I'm making note of them."

Some of the tension in him disappeared. "Good. Really, really good. And I'm glad that you're handling this investigation and not me."

"Yeah, well, if Mom is right, don't count yourself out too soon. We just might be investigating two sides of the same case."

He gulped. "Great. Hopefully, when we meet in the middle, we won't have to deal with that." He pointed to the screen.

"Totally agree." Then I sniffed the air. It was a testament to just how much what I was watching bothered me, that I only just then noticed the delicious aroma drifting up from downstairs.

Carny's pizza. Definitely time for a break.

I paused the horrible video, as I'd still have to finish watching it for the cause, and closed my laptop. But when I pushed the chair back from the desk and went to stand up, Opie stopped me.

Raising one eyebrow, I tilted my head at him. "You're seriously getting between me and Carny's pizza? You do know I can take you, right?"

He nodded. "Oh, yeah. In a multitude of ways too. Always could." Then his grin faded as he looked into my eyes. "But I think we need to talk."

Nothing good ever came out of those words, did it? With my heart in my throat, I kept my mouth firmly shut. I'm not big on delaying bad news.

"Patricia will be here for at least a couple of weeks. I think it might be a good idea if I go back to my apartment until she's ready to be on her own again."

I'd say I shook my head, but the violent back and forth motion my head was making was so much more than a simple shake. "You are NOT leaving me to deal with Patricia Bluespring alone. No way, no how." I glanced at the open office door and lowered my voice. "You realize what's at stake with her and me in such close quarters, don't you? I really need you here as a buffer."

"I won't be here during the day anyway, and I think it will be more comfortable for Patricia without having a man in the house. Especially if she's going to have to bathe in the bloody living room."

Ah, privacy. So that was what this was about.

I glanced into the room off the office. Liz's bedroom. Patricia couldn't use it because of the stairs, but if we moved it into the dining room downstairs that we didn't use anyway, she could.

"If that is all this is about, why don't we take tonight and move a little furniture. As long as Liz is okay with loaning out her bed, we can shove the dining room table and chairs to one side and fit the bed in there with no trouble." I paused to give him time to think it through. "The dining room has doors, so she'd have privacy. A room all to herself."

Good thing Liz's bed was a twin size.

He still wasn't fully on board with my plan, so I pulled out the final show stopper. The danger card.

"Besides, don't you think having a man in the house will help us out, safety-wise? Especially with that man being an officer of the law. Should make the shooter think twice about trying anything while she's here, shouldn't it?"

That did the trick, as I'd known it would.

He blew out a long breath and finally gave me a nod. Then he leaned over and put his forehead to mine. "Okay, but don't think I don't know that there's more to it than this. What's really bugging you? I know you don't like Patricia, but I'm sensing there's more to it than that."

I swallowed. "There is. She could take this place back, you know. Legally, we don't stand a chance against her, according to Dad. I'm afraid that the longer she stays, and the more comfortable we make her, the bigger the chances are that she'll do just that."

My vision was getting a little fuzzy. Probably because of the dang water in my eyes. I'd so had my hopes of me and Opie raising a family in this house. Our own version of the Ravenswind farmhouse.

He brushed his lips against mine gently and wiped one of the leaking tears off my cheek. "You know we can be together anywhere, right? I'm not here because of the house. I'm here because you're here. Wherever you are will be home to me."

I blinked back the tears and sniffed. "Promise?"

"Cross my heart. And if this place doesn't work out, then we'll find another one. Together."

Together.

That sounded really nice.

***

Luckily, the others had saved us a pizza. Although I caught Arc's eyes glancing toward our box more than once. When had he come over? Those videos must have had me even more distracted than I'd thought.

As I took my first garlic and marinara infused bite, we heard the vehicle pull into the drive.

"That would be Lily," Mom said, heading for the door.

"Lily?" I glanced at Patricia, but she was still nibbling on her last slice of pizza, making it last. I can't say as I blamed her. She didn't seem to have any trouble with the extra company, so I shrugged and finished my bite.

"Yes, dear. I hadn't been thinking earlier. Archie's car isn't big enough to fit that old washtub in. So I asked Lily to bring it by for us. Her van comes in so handy sometimes."

I had to give her that. As my current vehicle was a tiny doodlebug, I knew all about space issues. Just grocery shopping could become a game of Tetris when I made it back to the store's parking lot with my haul.

But if Lily with the magic hammer was here, moving that bed would be so much easier. And I was sure we had a hammer in that nifty little toolbox that Opie had set up for us.

I told the others of the possible plan to move Liz's bed downstairs, and the idea got a rousing agreement. Liz seemed pleased too.

Liz looked at Patricia with big eyes. "Would you mind if I brought down the blow-up mattress too? We could pretend it was a slumber party. Like we had when we were kids."

Patricia grinned at her. "Sounds good to me." She motioned down at her leg. "If nothing else, this will give us a chance to catch up a whole lot better." Then she caught my eye. "When I'm not working on the computer and making calls, of course."

Dang straight. Family reunions were nice and all, but we were all on a mission for the Goddess. This wasn't something I could do alone.

Then I thought about it. Patricia was right. For the next couple of weeks, she would be limited as to just how much investigating she could do. Fieldwork would be out of the question unless of course, she could get the field to come to her. Not sure how I felt about that. This was my home, and I wanted to keep it safe. Well, it was my home for now, anyway.

"If you need me to go out and interview someone or run something down for you, just let me know," I offered.

She gave me a surprised look. "Thanks. I may have to take you up on that."

"I can help with that too, you know," Ruby said, slightly flexing her muscles so that the outfit would be more apparent. "I'm kind of good at that kind of thing. Not that Amie isn't, of course."

I'd better watch out. The next thing I knew, Ruby would try to partner in my investigations too. Although, now that I think about it, we might make a good team. Kind of like cloning myself, but without having to worry about stressing out Opie too much. I really didn't think he could handle two of me.

One was hard enough.

While Lily worked on getting the bed torn down and put back up, and the men worked on carrying out the dining room table and chairs, we set up a kind of investigation headquarters in the living room. It kind of made sense.

All three of us were working on the same job, after all. Well, four if you counted Mom, but she would go back with Lily. So, yeah, three of us. Who knows?

Maybe by the end of all this, I'd trust Patricia enough to come clean with her.

I highly doubted that would be the case, but it was possible. Barely, but possible.

We shoved a couple of chairs into another room to make room for the dining room table. That could serve as our central working station. Each of us would have plenty of room to set up their computers and even notebooks and other needed supplies.

And we'd all be together to help each other. If one of us learned something juicy, the others would know seconds later.

I was starting to think this could be an interesting way to do things. Investigation in tandem. And yes, I meant interesting in a good way. Normally it was rather a lonely occupation.

Of course, I'd have to make a trip back to Patricia's tomorrow to pick up her laptop. We'd all been a little too focused on just Athena the first trip. I hate that I had been so shortsighted. Even I should have thought enough to grab her more clothes and her computer.

Although, truthfully, her computer had probably been in her office, which would have made bringing it difficult to do without going against her wishes.

Mom and Lily were getting ready to head out when I turned to them. "I know Patricia isn't ready to be on her own, but just how much can she do? Would she be able to go with me to her house to grab some things?"

She hesitated. "Not for a few days at least, dear. I'm thinking the motion of the car ride wouldn't be good for the healing process." She glanced pointedly at the table we had set up and pretty much ready to go. "And I don't think it's a great idea for her to be up sitting for long periods of time, either. That leg needs to be elevated most of the time."

"That's okay," Patricia piped in from the couch. "I can work from here with the lap desk. We'll still be in the same room."

I took a deep breath and nodded. "Okay, then, we have a plan of attack. The only thing is, we have three people and two computers. I was planning to go back to Patricia's to pick up some things for her tomorrow, but with her office being off-limits… well, I'm betting I couldn't grab her laptop."

Patricia looked conflicted, but before she had to come to a hard decision, Opie came to her rescue.

"She can use mine during the day. I only need it at night, anyway."

She looked at him gratefully. "Thank you. That means a lot."

He shrugged. "Why don't you all come and look at the new downstairs bedroom?" He glanced over at me. "It's something we might want to keep for guests who have trouble climbing stairs."

A quick glance at Patricia showed even more confliction on her face.

Yeah, we were so going to lose this place.

Opie didn't seem to like the idea of me going to Patricia's the next day without him. As he'd already promised his dad not to ditch work on Sunday, that meant a later night drive over and back.

Probably worked out for the best, anyway. Patricia and Ruby swore that they could handle getting the washtub filled up, and I knew for a fact that Ruby would have no trouble heating the water for her once it was filled. I figured Arc would be doing a lot of the filling up part of it. But then they could shuffle him back to the barn and the two women could take it from there.

And Opie wouldn't have to worry about the whole privacy thing. A win-win situation, if ever there was one.

We got the list of things that Patricia wanted, along with their locations in the cabin. Not that we should have any trouble finding them. There were not a lot of places to look.

The dresser by her bed held all the clothes, and the tiny bathroom had everything else on her list. We were in and out in under five minutes.

Probably much faster than the man in the shadows outside had expected.

Chapter 14

I sensed something was wrong the instant we stepped out Patricia's front door. From the sudden tension in Opie, I was guessing he sensed it too. He reached out and squeezed my hand, not wanting to say anything for fear of giving our knowledge of being watched away. I squeezed back to let him know I was on board.

Sometimes it would be really nice to have that mental communication I had with Destiny extend to Opie. This was one of them.

The problem was, we didn't know if the person in the shadows had a gun or not. That simple little fact made a huge difference to us.

If it was the shooter, which was our first guess, then the answer was most likely yes.

"We forgot her toothbrush," Opie said. "Why don't you go back and get it?"

I stared at him. Like I was going back into the cabin and leaving him out here like a sitting duck. "Why don't you show me where she keeps it?"

Even in the dark, I could tell he was gritting his teeth. Well, he knew what he was getting into when he chose me for a mate. I wasn't the meek, docile kind of girl to let my man risk his life to save me. I was more the type to don the armor and save myself. Him too, for that matter.

Armor. Huh. Now there was an idea. If that spell of mine could hold back the force of an explosion, surely it could slow down a bullet. And, I would think, greatly lessen the damage.

When my hair started floating, Opie's eyes widened. Once the spell was in place, I shouted, "Go!"

We ran to the spot where the watcher was hiding. Whether our move surprised the heck out of them or they really weren't armed, I didn't know at the time. But the important thing was my spell wasn't tested. No flying bullets.

Instead, there was a slightly masculine sounding "Eek!" and the man tried to run. He didn't get far. Old men can't run all that fast.

Old witches not used to running, run even slower.

"Ow! Get off of me, you big overgrown buffoon!"

Crapsnackles.

I knew that voice. Could it really be this easy?

I tapped Opie on the shoulder. "I think it's safe. You can let him up, but if one hair on his head starts to float, you have my full permission to zap him with the taser gun."

Wild eyes looked up at me from the ground. "You have a taser?"

Yeah, not so cocky now, huh? I didn't think there'd be any more problems out of the man. Not now that he knew what the stakes here truly were. No one wants to have that much electricity slammed into them.

No one sane anyway. I was hoping the word sane applied to Gaston Crowe. Right now, though, all bets on that were off.

"What are you doing here watching Patricia's cabin, Gaston?"

Opie looked at me as the man slowly stood up and brushed himself off. "You know him?"

I nodded and even raised an eyebrow in an attempt to make my words even more poignant. "Oh yes. He's a member of our illustrious witches' council."

Opie's eyes flashed back to the man now leaning against a rather large tree, rubbing his back. "I see." I could tell by his voice that he was on board with the full implications of the current situation.

We had a possibly evil council member lurking in the shadows outside of Patricia's cabin. Didn't look good for poor old Gaston. But if we could have this whole thing wrapped up in a matter of a few hours, I would be one happy little camper.

"First of all, I'm Councilman Crowe to you, Ms. Ravenswind," he said, stretching to his full height. "And I don't see the need to answer any of your questions. You have no authority over me. But I, however, do have authority over you. And I would very much like to know what you were doing inside Patricia's home."

Opie laughed, and Gaston gave him an angry stare. "I see nothing funny from my stand."

"Is he for real?" Opie asked me. "We have him dead to rights, and he's playing like he's holding all the cards?"

I nodded. That was Gaston to a tee, unfortunately. Just then, a cruel breeze shifted the hair at the back of my neck and sent a shiver down my spine. "Why don't we go inside and have a little talk where it's not freezing?" Then I took another look at the man in front of us. "Why are you not shaking like a leaf? It's bloody cold out here."

His chin raised. "Witches—well, most of us—have magic, you know. It's a fairly simple spell to give oneself a personal boundary of warmth."

Huh. Something I should definitely look into.

And it answered one of my main questions too. Now I knew why Gaston hadn't blasted us with a spell to give himself time to get away. He'd been too busy holding the warmth spell in place.

Not so smart after all, huh? But I didn't think he'd like it so much if I pointed that out. For once I let diplomat Amie win, and I kept my trap shut.

Once inside the cabin, Gaston's eyes traveled quickly over everything. Then they landed on the duffel bag that I'd brought in from the porch where we'd left it in our rush to get to Gaston.

"What are you taking from Patricia?" Gaston asked. Then he shook his head. "Scratch that. Most important questions first. What have you done with her? Have you hurt her?" His eyes flared as he spoke.

It was hard to fake that kind of thing. All of a sudden, I had a deep unsettling feeling that Gaston wasn't our bad guy. I should have known it couldn't end this easily.

"Patricia is safe." I looked over at Opie. "I'd kind of like to make a phone call before we tell him too much."

Opie nodded. "Good idea. After all, she's the one in danger right now."

Gaston looked from one of us to the other and back again, but he didn't say anything. He was waiting. Maybe I could learn a thing or two from him.

I popped out my cellphone and dialed Patricia. When she answered, I gave her a brief rundown of what was going on. Then I asked the important question. "Do you think it's safe to tell him what happened?"

There was a moment's silence on the other end of the call. "Not all of it, no. Keep the personal information out of it." I was gathering she wasn't going to say the wolf word over the phone for a few different reasons. I didn't blame her, either. "I think we can tell him I've been shot, but not fatally, and that I'm temporarily staying with you." Another pause and her voice sounded very sincere when she spoke next. "I don't have many friends on the council, Amie. Gaston and your aunt may be the only two. I really hope he isn't mixed up in this."

"So do I. I'll call you back when I know more." I took a lesson from Opie's conversations with his dad and just hung up. Then I turned back to Gaston. "Okay, she says we can tell you what's happened. As it involved her, I wanted her input first."

For the first time, Gaston looked unsure. "That was Patricia you were talking to?"

"It was. She says you're a friend. I hope she isn't wrong about that."

He swallowed and looked away. "She is not wrong." He paused and then pulled out the counter stool and sat heavily. "That's why I'm here. I tried calling her all last night and early this morning, then my blasted phone died. I traced her to a park, but the trail vanished there. I was afraid..." His voice trailed off.

I stared at him, my mind racing. It made sense. If I'd been worried about someone I loved, or even really, really liked, and they disappeared, the first thing I'd do would be a find spell. From the sound of it, when Patricia the human changes into Patricia the wolf, the trail ends. And since she had made the trip to our place as a wolf, there would have been nothing for him to follow to find her.

All good information to know.

It just didn't get us any closer to solving this thing.

"Wait a minute. Why were you so worried about her? For all you knew, she just hooked up with someone and spent the night at their place."

He just stared at me. "Patricia Bluespring

wouldn't do that. If you think otherwise, then perhaps you are lying about knowing her at all."

I glanced over at Opie, who shrugged. Big help he was.

"Well, we aren't all that close, but I was the closest one at hand when she needed help, so she turned to me. That has to mean she trusts me at least a little, right?"

"She needed help?" He sat up on the edge of the stool. "What's happened to her?"

I told him. All of it, minus the werewolf part. I couldn't come up with any other reason for his finding spell to end at the park, so I just left that out too. That would be up to Patricia to explain.

In the end, he was staring at me with wide eyes and a horrified expression. Then his face settled into stony determination. "You will take me to her. I need to see her for myself."

"Sorry, but it's far too late tonight, and my man... ouch." The ouch was because Opie had just elbowed me hard in the side.

"You can come to visit Patricia tomorrow." Opie paused. "Or, better still, you can charge your phone and call her yourself."

Gaston looked from Opie to me. He didn't look happy about that, but he couldn't very well force us to take him, now could he? Bottom line, even as powerful as he was, I was fairly certain I could take him in a magic fight.

Not that it would come to that. Opie would taser him the instant the hair started flying. He was just that way. Smart man.

Gaston crossed his arms against his chest. "I'm not leaving until I have personally spoken with Patricia." He stared pointedly at my phone.

I blew out a breath and handed it to him. "Fine.

Call her."

He looked at the phone and then back to me. His face grew a tad bit red. "I don't recall her number."

"She's the last one I called, just redial that call."

It took him a minute, but he did it. Gaston Crowe was obviously not all that good with technology. A lot of older witches had the same problem. They hated relying on anything but their magic. But magic didn't make long-distance calls. At least, not the spells I knew.

Their conversation was short and rather cryptic on this end. Even with his pointed stares and head jerks, I wasn't leaving the cabin to make his call a more private one. For one, it was my phone he was using, and for another, it was bloody well cold outside.

Finally, he ended the call and handed me back my phone. Then he stood and walked to the door.

"So that's it, then?" I asked. "No thank you very much. No goodbye?"

He looked over his shoulder at me, not even bothering to turn around. "I'll see you tomorrow. As you say, it's late tonight." And he walked out the door and disappeared into the darkness.

I listened for a minute, but I didn't hear the sound of a motor starting up. "Do you think he walked here?"

Opie shrugged. His shoulders were getting a workout tonight. "He does have that warmth spell." His eyes got thoughtful. "Don't suppose that's something you could learn? And maybe cast on friends and family?"

I grinned up at him. "I'm so ahead of you on that one."

We locked the cabin back up and got in the car to head home. Home. That sounded so nice right now. I wasn't even going to allow myself to think that change might come soon on that front. It was home, dang it all.

We were halfway home before I thought to ask him why he'd elbowed me.

"You were about to tell Gaston that I worked tomorrow, weren't you?"

"Well, yeah. So?"

"So, I didn't think it would be a very smart thing to do, considering he is a major suspect."

I raised an eyebrow at him. "You still think he might be the one who shot Patricia?"

He nodded.

"Why?"

"He was wearing Doctor Scholls hiking shoes."

My breath caught in my throat as I recalled Opie's earlier shopping and investigation run. I took it to mean that the shooter was a fan of Doctor Scholls footwear.

"Oh." I mean, what more was there to say?

Other than the fact that I'd just invited a possible would-be killer to my home in the morning.

Crapsnackles.

Chapter 15

The others were already tucked into bed when we got home. Or, at least, I assumed they were. Ruby, Arc, Lily, and Mom were nowhere to be seen, so the assumption was that they'd headed to their respective homes and beds.

Patty was off the couch, and the dining room door was firmly shut. Part of me wanted to check on her, but part wanted to respect her privacy. It was a conundrum. It wasn't like there was a lock on the dining-room door. But it would kind of defeat the purpose of giving her a separate downstairs bedroom if I just ignored the closed door and walked in.

So, I called her.

"What?" Not a fantastic, nor friendly, way to answer the phone, that. "I know you're home because I heard you come in."

"Good. I just wanted to make sure you were safe and sound before heading up to bed. And I need to know what you want me to do with the things we brought from your place."

There was a slight hesitation. "Sorry. Just put them by the door to my room. I'll get them the next time I go to the bathroom."

"About that," I said, really hating to say the next few words. "Is that something you can handle on your own? Or should I sleep on the couch in case you need me?" I'll admit, my fingers were crossed hard that she would say no.

She chuckled. "Go to bed, Amie. I should be fine, but I'll call you if I need anything. Now, do you have anything else to say before I finally drift off to sleep?"

"Well, you should know that Gaston will be here sometime tomorrow. He wasn't all that keen on taking my word that you were all right."

"That sounds like him. Thanks." Another pause. "And thanks for everything else, too, in case I haven't said it before. My new room is nice."

I swallowed and had to force out a goodnight. I was really hoping I hadn't made a mistake in letting her get comfortable in my house. Maybe I should have left her on the couch after all.

Opie must have read my mind because his arm came over my shoulders, and he guided me toward and up the stairs. "Whatever happens, it will be okay. You know that, right?"

"Yeah." I squeezed a little tighter into his side. "As long as I have you, that is." But having him and the house would be even better.

***

The alarm went off far too early the next morning. I tried to roll over and ignore it. After all, it was for Opie, not for me.

"Don't you think you need to get the day started too?" He asked, poking me.

I snuggled deeper into the covers. That should have answered his question right there. Unfortunately, he didn't give up quite so easily.

"Come on, sleepyhead. There's a lot of work to

be done, and you're going to have to play hostess at least part of the day. You aren't going to want to do that on an empty stomach, now are you? Gaston struck me as the type to be an early riser."

Crapsnackles. I hated it when he made such good points so very early in the morning.

"All right, all right. I'm getting up. Satisfied?"

He laughed. "I'll be more satisfied when I see you actually on your feet."

What a slave driver. I took a deep breath and pushed the covers to one side. When the cold hit my bare legs, I got moving a little faster. At least until I got my robe on. That's when I got my first good look at Opie. He was fully dressed and ready to go.

Huh. I could have sworn the alarm just went off.

"I got up a little early this morning. I have a stop I want to make on the way to work."

I tilted my head at him. Then I decided that if it was important, he'd be telling me anyway, so I let that go. I walked over to him and gave him a peck on the lips. "Be careful today, okay?"

He pulled me in tight and kissed me. "Right back at you, kid."

"You do know we're the same age, right?"

He grinned at me. "Only in earthly years, my love." Then he took my hand and started pulling me toward the bedroom door. "Walk me out."

I eyed the bathroom, and he laughed again. "Okay, but make it snappy. I don't want to have shortened my sleep for nothing."

Within a minute, I was back at his side. It doesn't take me long to do the necessary things after a short night's sleep. I was hoping for an early night tonight. Or better yet, a little afternoon nap. Opie would never have to know, would he?

At the front door, Opie pulled me in for another,

deeper kiss. Then he looked down at me before letting me go. "The wards are still good, right?"

"Oh, yeah. Lily tested and approved, too, which says a lot. No one with ill intent toward any of us will get into the house."

He hesitated. "That still stands even if you invite them in, right?"

"Yup. If Gaston is our bad guy, he won't be able to step one foot inside our front door." Now that I thought about it, that wasn't a bad way to test out his innocence. If only we could come up with some way to get all the council members to come over, we'd have this settled in nothing flat.

"Good." His eyes bore into mine. "But keep your taser handy all the same, okay?"

I smiled at him. I loved how he sometimes forgot I was one of the most powerful witches on the face of the earth. "Promise."

He had opted for a remote start on his vehicle, so it was already running, defrosted, and ready to go when he climbed inside. It was too dark to see him at the wheel past his headlights, but I waved all the same as he made his turn to go down the drive. "Goddess, keep him safe today and bring him home to me unharmed," I whispered.

"You two really are in love, aren't you?"

I jumped at the voice that came from directly over my shoulder. Whirling, I saw Patricia standing just a couple of feet from me.

"Sorry," she said. "I didn't want to interrupt your goodbyes, but I need the bathroom. Don't suppose you'd be willing to give me a little support?"

From the tone of her voice, I could tell how much she hated asking for help. "No problem."

I maneuvered under her shoulder and let her lean on me as we walked to the bathroom. At the door, I paused.

"I can take it from here." She hesitated. "Give me a lift back in a few?"

"I'll wait right here for you."

She nodded and stepped in, closing the door behind her. I didn't hear the lock engage, so at least she was being smart about things. If she had trouble in there, I'd need to be able to get to her without taking down the blasted door in the process.

A few scant minutes later, she was back. I noticed she was leaning a lot heavier on me this trip. Patricia might not want the world to know it, but she wasn't quite as strong as she liked to think she was. At least, not after being shot.

She stopped at the couch. "Would you mind if I crashed here?"

"Fine by me. I'll even fix us something to eat." I helped her get settled, then looked at her. She was wearing a pair of long flannel pajamas. So much more practical for this time of year than my simple oversized T-shirt. "Were you wanting to get dressed now, or wait a bit?"

She thought about it, then shook her head. "I think I'll wait a bit." A grimace crossed her face. "I don't suppose you have any pain meds you'd be willing to share?"

A quick trip to our medicine cabinet later, I handed her two pills and a glass of water. "Here you go. Take these, and then I'll try my hand at boosting Mom's healing spell. Fair warning, I'm not as good as her at it." Hence the pills.

She just stared at me with one eyebrow raised. Oh yeah, I'd kind of forgotten that the rest of the world of witches still thought I had little to no magic. Not exactly something I wanted to change, either. I'd have to play this carefully.

"That is, if you're willing?"

Another pain-filled grimace. "I'm willing... if you know what you're doing."

I took a deep breath and gave her a nod. "Mom's been working with me. Like I said, I'm not nearly as good at it as she is, but then who is?"

Patricia laid back on the couch like she expected my touch to hurt more than it helped. Not a great confidence booster that. I pulled in some magic, just a trickle, and touched her leg. "My strength and health I loan to thee, be of good faith and pain will flee."

I let the trickle of magic pass from my fingertips into Patricia's leg. At her sudden start, I paused.

"No, don't stop. That feels like heaven."

Uh-oh. A bit too much. I pulled back on the trickle, basically halving the magic I was using. After another second or two, I ended the spell.

"How does that feel?"

She sighed and closed her eyes. "If you were a man, I'd marry you right here on the spot. I think you've found your calling, Amie. Your mother just might need to be watching her back."

Not the reaction I wanted at all. But at least she didn't seem to be questioning it too much. I was hoping she wouldn't start once the euphoria of being pain-free wore off.

"Do you prefer your cereal more on the sugary side or healthy side?" Sue me, but I would not start cooking for her. Besides, it was far too early for me to be standing at a stove.

"Today? Sugary works for me."

I fixed two bowls of sugary goodness and brought them into the living room. We ate in blessed silence. At least she wasn't one to want to carry on a conversation while eating. I appreciated that. Food was very important to me.

When we finished, I rinsed out the bowls and the silverware and placed them in the dish rack to dry. No fancy dishwasher for me. I liked things simple, and besides, I didn't really trust a machine to get them clean, so I'd be basically washing the dishes before putting them in, anyway. Silly, I know, but me.

"Opie said Gaston was probably an early riser. How early do you think that would be?" I asked as I walked back into the living room.

The words had no sooner left my mouth than the knock came. Patricia barked out a laugh. "That answer your question?"

Yeah, pretty much. But when I looked out the door, it wasn't only Gaston Crowe standing there. He'd brought reinforcements. In the way of my Aunt Opal. I gulped.

She did not look happy.

Chapter 16

I forced a smile and opened the door. "Hello, Auntie. I wasn't expecting you."

She grunted. "No doubt, as you didn't bother to call and tell me what the devil was going on. I had to hear it from Gaston here. You would have thought my own flesh and blood would have forewarned me, wouldn't you?"

I had a couple of options on how to play this. I could take full blame and the accompanying licks, or I could totally throw my cousin Ruby under the bus.

Giving her the sweetest smile I could muster, I said, "Oh, I'm so sorry! I totally would have called, but I assumed Ruby told you."

Opal gave me the Ravenswind stare. From her, it was super intimidating. She'd perfected the thing. "Don't worry, I'll get to my daughter later. In the future, call me." She stepped in through the threshold, but Gaston just stood there, waiting.

What was he, a vampire? At first that thought was a bit funny, then not so much as I realized that I was currently housing a werewolf in my home. I swallowed and looked him in the eye. Most probably he was simply applying good manners. Right? That, or he couldn't enter for an entirely different reason. Like my wards.

"Please, Ga..., I mean Mr. Crowe, come in." I

made a sweeping motion indicating the same, and finally, he stepped in. I'll admit I breathed a little easier after he had crossed the threshold. I trusted my wards.

"Thank you."

"I didn't expect you to bring my aunt with you."

He just looked at me. "Well, you failed to give me an address, directions, or your phone number, so I had little choice but to call Opal. However, tagging along for the ride was totally her idea."

I'll bet that was the gospel truth. I couldn't believe I hadn't told him where to find us. As if everyone in the world knew right where we lived. Truthfully, though, what surprised me the most was that Opie hadn't caught my goof and corrected it. I counted on him for little things like that. He was totally slipping.

"Sorry about that. My mind was elsewhere last night."

He nodded shortly. "Hence the bringing of your aunt."

Yeah, about that. I sent another slightly worried glance to her right hand. She was holding a rather large bag. I was hoping that it wasn't Opal's version of an overnight bag. And if it was, I was really hoping that she planned to sleep over at Ruby and Arc's versus here. My house was quickly filling up, and I was officially out of beds already.

The sleeping arrangements were just the tip of the troublesome iceberg. Having Opal in the house meant a whole lot more. It was different at the farmhouse, where I had my own tiny apartment to go to and be alone. Here, things were much more open.

She saw my glance. "Don't you go worrying about the bag. We'll discuss that once we've taken care of Gaston." She glanced over at him. "It's a family matter."

He didn't seem to be upset about being left out

for that discussion. Actually, his eyes hadn't left the couch, and Patricia, since he first walked in the door.

"May I talk to her, please?"

I was confused at first. It wasn't like I'd told him he couldn't. If he was going to expect an invitation for every little move in my house, this could be a long and tiresome visit. Maybe I could shorten that a bit.

"Please, Mr. Crowe, make yourself at home. Visit with Patricia for as long as you like. The bathroom is that door over there." I pointed to make it even clearer. "And if you need anything, please just ask."

He gave another super brief nod and walked past me to the couch. Patricia stood to greet him.

That got a smile. The first one I'd ever seen on Gaston's face. It was a nice smile, but kind of disturbing all the same.

"So you truly are all right?"

She returned his smile. "Yes, Gaston. I'm so sorry I put you through worry." She opened her arms, and he stepped in for a brief hug. Another shock to my system. I was seeing a side of Gaston Crowe that I had never seen before. And I was starting to realize that the other members of the witches' council were more than just faces and names. They were human too. Somehow, I hadn't been expecting that.

He stood back and glanced at her from head to toe. "Amethyst said you'd been shot?"

"Yes, but luckily in the leg." She put her hand down over the hidden wound. "Also luckily, the bullet went straight through and didn't hit anything major."

"And no infection of any kind?"

"Knock on wood, not yet, at any rate." She smiled over at me. "Amie and her mother are crackerjack healers."

Opal raised an eyebrow at me. I lifted a shoulder. I knew I was supposed to keep my new powers secret, but I really had dialed it back—or at least tried to—and Mom had told me to keep up the healing in her absence.

Once we were all settled in, I sent Liz to get Ruby. I really couldn't imagine leaving her out of all the early morning fun. Why should she get to sleep in when I couldn't?

While we waited for them to walk over, I ran upstairs and threw on jeans and a shirt. I felt a lot more able to handle my present situation once I was out of my t-shirt and robe ensemble.

After everyone coming was present, Patricia turned to Gaston. "Why were you looking for me in the first place? I've only been gone a little over twenty-four hours."

"Which is a lot longer than you are usually gone, isn't it? You keep a pretty regular schedule."

She tilted her head at him. "That didn't answer my question, and you bloody well know it."

His face reddened, and he glanced at me and my family in consternation. "I don't suppose the two of us could have a little privacy?"

Opal saved me from having to answer. "I'm sorry, Gaston, but it would seem we are all involved in whatever the heck is going on here, and I for one intend to be present when information is shared."

He took a deep breath. "I was afraid that would be the answer." He looked back at Patricia. "Is it safe to talk? Or should we wait until you are home?"

She gave him a lopsided smile. "I trust the Ravenswinds and the Minehearts one hundred percent."

Liar, liar, pants on fire. But I wasn't going to tell him that.

"Well, then, as this is largely to do with you, I'll trust your judgment," he said, leaning toward her. "I was looking for you because I think we share a common worry." He nodded to her leg. "One that just might have gotten you shot."

Patricia's eyebrows shot up. "Exactly what worry are you speaking of?"

He darted another concerned glance at the rest of us, then finally, out of sheer desperation, it would seem, blurted it out. "Something is going on in the council. Something not good."

The rest of us shared a glance. The Goddess hadn't cleared Gaston, so as far as we were concerned, he was still a suspect. Actually, with him admitting to watching Patricia coupled with his choice of walking shoes, he was currently my prime suspect.

The trouble was, if he was the one to blame, he was a darn fine actor. I really think he cared about Patricia and her well-being. Which, in turn, made his suspecthood seem a lot less likely. Plus, there was the whole getting past the wards thing. That meant a lot right there.

From the look on Opal and Ruby's faces, I could tell they were thinking along the same lines I was. And I hadn't even had the chance to fill them in yet about the shoe thing.

"Why would you be coming to see me? Do you think I'm involved?"

Gaston shook his head. "I know you've been asking questions. Good questions. Questions that need to be answered. That's why I've been watching you. I wanted to offer my help, but didn't know how to go about it." He paused and hung his head. "Perhaps if I had offered my assistance sooner, this would not have happened."

Patricia closed her eyes and leaned back. "It is quite possible that my being shot has nothing to do with the council. It could be something else entirely."

He looked confused. "Like what?"

I leaned in. This was getting interesting.

"Unfortunately, I'm not at liberty to say. Suffice it to know that it does not concern witches in general or the council in particular."

I held my breath, waiting. Surely Gaston would press the issue, right?

Wrong. He gave a knowing nod. "I can accept that. However, do you truly think that is the case? That this incident is not council related?"

She opened her eyes again and met his gaze head-on. "At this point, I don't have a clue, to be honest. I just wanted you to know that it is possible for it not to be related to my council investigations."

He scooted a little closer to the edge of his seat. Much further and he'd be landing on the floor. I really hoped that didn't happen. I didn't think he'd take my laughter well. And if it happened, there is absolutely no way I could contain myself. It might be the stress of the current situation, but I was fighting a case of the giggles hard, just thinking about the possibility.

Not a good sign.

"Exactly what are you investigating? And why?"

She smiled and shook her head. "I'm on a mission, Gaston. A Goddess-given mission. Why don't you go first? What do you think is going on in the council?"

Yet another glance around the room at all of us watching and listening in.

"I'd prefer to have this conversation in private," he said, his gaze lingering just that extra few seconds on Opal.

"Or for Goddess' sake, Gaston," Opal said disgustedly. "If you haven't already guessed it, which apparently is the case, Patricia and I are working together on this. I'm on the same mission she is." She nodded over at me and Ruby too. "As are they. It's probably one reason she turned to my family in her time of need."

Gaston raised an eyebrow and looked to Patricia for confirmation. "Is this true?"

Opal snorted as Patricia gave him a nod.

"I'm not in the habit of telling falsehoods, Gaston, and you bloody well know it."

He nodded slowly. "It is true that I have never heard of Opal Ravenswind telling a lie. But whatever is going on in the council is also a never heard of situation. Isn't it?"

Opal grunted. "You have me there. But I still don't lie. I might not tell you the whole truth, or offer up all the information I have. But I won't lie."

Gaston mulled that over for a minute. "Fine. I will accept that as truth."

"You'd bloody well better because it is."

"Now that we've established that Opal doesn't lie and that I am working along with the Ravenswinds on this... something that if you think about it and you are right in this all being connected puts them in danger too... could you please answer my question? What do you think is going on in the council?"

He took a deep breath. Then he took another. Just when I'd given up hope of getting an answer out of him, he spoke.

"I think the council is draining magic from its members."

Opal bolted upright out of her chair. "Draining magic? How, and more importantly, who?"

I noticed that the one question my aunt didn't ask was what made him think that. That, in itself, had me more than a little worried.

"That's the problem. I don't know who or how. I'd convinced myself I was wrong and mistaken." He looked at Patricia. "Until I heard some of the questions you were asking. Questions that might just answer my own."

If Opal would not ask the main question, someone had to. I'd just opened my mouth to do so when Ruby beat me to the punch.

"Can we back up a minute here? What makes you think the council is draining magic?" she asked.

He looked at her and then back to Patricia, who nodded. This was getting more than tiresome. "Magic doesn't fade with age, you know. In the past, it has always gotten stronger with the passing years. That has changed." He wouldn't meet anyone's eyes, not even Patricia's. "My magic is weakening. For the first time in my life, I am starting to have trouble casting spells that I used to be able to do with ease. That isn't right. As the world is still turning, and the Goddess still allowing us to draw breath, my thoughts and suspicions go to the council."

"The council has always required a sample of magic from each of its members to be held in the library," Opal said slowly.

They what? That was news to me. "What kind of sample?"

"A crystal filled with magic. A stored spell, if you will," Gaston said thoughtfully. It was pretty obvious that he was considering the implications of that and the current situation. "It's their way of keeping tabs on us. Having our magical signatures right there at their fingertips. A good way to trace what we are doing with our magic."

My eyes widened. "They can trace your magic through the sample?"

Opal nodded. "Yes. And although it pains me to no end to admit this, I have felt my magic ebbing a bit lately as well. Though it never occurred to me that it could be council related." She gave Gaston a respectful glance. "It was highly intuitive of you to make that connection. Well done."

He blushed and lifted one shoulder. "I'm not entirely certain of it, you know. It could be something else entirely. But when I overheard Patricia asking questions, something inside me just clicked. I think there is something there."

"Oh, there is something there all right," Opal said. "Patricia wasn't lying about that Goddess-given part of our mission. She knows something is going on in the council, and now you've given us a very good place to center our investigations. Thank you."

Gaston raised an eyebrow at her. "You say that as if you are dismissing me. That is not the case. All of you may well be on a Goddess-given mission. I will not dispute that, as I know little to nothing about your Goddess. However, I too am on a mission. One given by the Great Spirit himself." He looked around the room, meeting each of our gazes. "Like it or not, it would seem prudent for all of us to work together on this."

I gulped. I wasn't sure how I felt about adding an unsanctioned member to our team. There was still the possibility in my mind that Gaston was a suspect rather than an ally. Granted, that possibility seemed to be dwindling fast, but it was still there.

Just how much could we trust him? I mean, come on, I still had doubts about Patricia and she had the Goddess' approval.

Even as my mind was still whirling, my tiny little Destiny leaped into Gaston's lap. Then she raised her front paws onto his chest and gazed up and into his eyes.

It took a minute for him to get past his surprise at her sudden and somewhat forceful appearance. Once that had passed, he met her gaze. They stared into each other's eyes for a long moment, during which Gaston gulped twice. None of us said a word. It was apparent that the Goddess was taking measures into her own hands.

Better her judgment than ours.

I glanced down and noticed that Athena was sitting at the foot of Gaston's chair, gazing up as well. They were double-teaming the poor man. It was almost enough to make me feel sorry for him.

Almost.

Chapter 17

There seemed to be a major battle of wills going on between my familiar and Gaston Crowe. For what it's worth, there wasn't a shred of doubt in my mind as to who the ultimate victor would be. I knew my cat.

Finally, after another few minutes of silent battle, Gaston broke. "Fine!"

Destiny, looking altogether too proud of herself, curled up in his lap and began purring. I might be mistaken, but I do believe the Goddess just gained another believer.

Gaston's eyes were more than a little bit wild when they sought out mine. "Your familiar is... quite a bit more than just a regular cat, isn't she?"

I grinned at him. "Oh, you noticed that, did you?"

He nodded and gulped. "Kind of hard to miss with a soul gaze like that." He started petting her absently, and the purring grew louder. "I think I feel better about trusting all of you now. If you have a cat this powerful, then you must truly be what you say you are." He swallowed again. "And I must say, I may have to change my beliefs regarding your Goddess. Until today, I'd always thought she was a bit... well... flighty."

Destiny's head popped up, and both she and Athena sneezed. It made him finally notice the white feline at his feet. "Oh my," he said, barely over a whisper. "There's another?"

"The one on the floor is my familiar, Athena, and yes, there are two." Patricia paused. "Well, actually, there are three, but one of them hasn't exactly joined in the fun yet. Not that we know of, anyway."

Opal shook her head. "The witch she belongs to is far too young to get messed up in this. I want to keep her safe and out of harm's way. Apparently, her familiar feels the same."

I hoped Opal was right on that. It might be a good thing to check in on Nancy more often than I had been of late. She might well tell me things she wouldn't tell her adoptive mother. Even as a loving mother, which Opal very much was, she was still intimidating as all get out.

"I see." Gaston was quiet for a minute. "All right then, I guess I should start by telling you a little about myself and my personal mission."

"That would be helpful, yes," Opal said dryly.

He glanced at her, then centered his gaze on the cat on his lap as he petted her. "You all should know by now that I don't consider myself a witch. I'm a shaman for my people."

Except for the fact that he was an upstanding member of the witches' council, that made sense. I knew he was a Native American. Anyone who took one glance at him would know that. Gaston was tall and slender, with beautiful perpetually tanned skin and long black hair that he wore in a single braid down his back. He could have modeled for a school textbook on the Cherokee tribe. The perfect modern-day example of a modern-day Cherokee Indian.

"So, what does a Shaman do, exactly?" I asked. I wasn't as up to date on all of that as I should be. I remember the term, but I got them confused with

Medicine Men. Or were they both the same thing?

"Shamans are healers. We use words and, yes, sometimes spells to protect and help our people."

I could feel my brows going together. "You do know that you've just described a witch, don't you?"

He sighed. "Yes. But to me, a Shaman is all that and more."

"What's the more part?" I asked.

He glared at me. "Well, until a few minutes ago, the more part was the fact that I served the Great Spirit while witches tend to serve a flighty Goddess that seems to fancy see-through clothing. Ouch! Easy with the claws."

I didn't even try to hide my smile as Gaston reached down to disengage Destiny's claws from his leg. Teach him to belittle the Goddess with her representatives right there in the same room. I wasn't just talking about the cats, either.

Each and every one of us was working under the Goddess' rule, and blessings too. We counted on it every single day.

"But now that you've seen the error in your way," Opal inserted, "Can you see that you are in fact a witch? Maybe a Native American witch, but a witch all the same?"

He nodded. "I suppose so. But I still prefer Shaman. It's more fitting with my heritage."

Opal inclined her head. "I can accept that." Funny how her words rather echoed Gaston's from earlier. "So has your Great Spirit given you any clues what is going on?"

He shook his head. "Not really. Just some of my dreams of late have centered on the council." A shiver passed over him. "The dreams have not been pleasant. Their meanings were clear, if not specific. There is something bad brewing in the council. That coupled with my ebbing power led to my magic draining theory."

We all looked at each other. That matched pretty much exactly what we'd been told too. It seemed that maybe Gaston was on our side after all.

"So, has your Goddess given you any clues?"

"Sadly, no. According to the Goddess, something is brewing in the council, but it's being hidden from her. The trouble is, hiding something from the Goddess herself would take a tremendous amount of magic," Opal said. "Which also aligns with your magic draining theory. We'd been wondering how they were getting the magic to keep their nasty little secret. Now, I think perhaps we know."

Gaston took a deep breath. "The question remains, what do we do about it? The part of the council's library that holds our collective magic isn't just open for all and sundry to visit. How do we find the witches responsible and stop them?"

"Well," I said slowly, drawing that one word out for all it was worth. "I think the first place to start would be with who exactly does have access to that part of the library. That seems the logical place to start to me."

The others just looked at me. "Well, isn't it?"

"Yes, but it isn't quite that simple. The library itself is a sacred place. While we aren't given leave to simply go and come throughout the entire facility as we chose to, every witch has limited access to it," Opal said slowly.

"But would that access be enough to give you time to use the spells to trace the magic and start pulling from it?" I asked.

"No, it would not."

"Then we're back to the question of who has full access to the library? Who does have the time and access they would need to pull something like this off?"

"I just want to say here, that I have no absolute

proof that this is, indeed, what is happening," Gaston said quietly. "I fear it is, but there is no proof."

"Agreed," Opal said. "But your theory is making incredibly good sense along with our limited knowledge of the situation. We owe you for bringing our thoughts to this."

"But even so, I feel we will need proof before going forward, don't you?" Gaston pressed, staring into Opal's eyes. "Especially considering who we are talking about?"

I let out a big breath and turned to Patricia. "While these two continue to ignore my question and talk amongst just the two of themselves, would you kindly tell me who has full access to the library?"

She gave them both a worried glance, but at least she was willing to give me the answer. "There are only three will full access. The leaders of the council, Crystal Waters and Tabitha Greenfield, and the librarian herself." She paused. "Actually, the librarian isn't technically a council member." Her eyes flew to Opal. "As such, she isn't on any of our investigation lists."

Crapsnackles. That was so not good.

***

We spent the next hour in a deep discussion with Gaston and the full Goddess investigation crew, minus my mom. Arc dismissed himself to attend to other things. Not that we were trying to exclude him, but there might have been a reason the Goddess hadn't included the Minehearts in the mission. We needed to respect that, even if we didn't understand it. For my part, I thought they just might be a big help. But so be it. Goddess rules.

Even with all that discussion, we didn't come up with much of a plan. The librarian was a witch, just not a council member. As such, she might be more accessible to us. Then again, maybe not. Her position was every bit as powerful as Crystal's was. When I thought of all that stored magic sitting there surrounding her day in and day out, I had to wonder if maybe she might not be the most powerful of all of us.

Especially if she was the one on the receiving end of the magic drain.

Once Gaston left, I thought we were through for a while. But when I stood to retreat upstairs to my little office slash library, Opal stopped me.

"Could I speak to you for a minute or two, please?"

It scared me that she'd used the please word. That was as close as Opal came to begging. And a begging Opal was something to worry about. A lot.

"Sure. Do you want to come up to my library with me? Maybe we can go over what I've got so far."

"Hey, not entirely fair to those of us not able to climb stairs, you know," Patricia said. "I thought that's why we set up the headquarters down here. So I wouldn't be excluded."

Opal smiled at her. "We'll come back down before start talking about the council, I promise." She looked at me. "This is more of a family matter."

Uh-oh. I didn't like the sound of that. I hoped everyone was still doing well. If Kimberly and Opal had had a falling out... or was the baby okay?

Opal must have seen the worry flash across my face. "Nothing terrible, Amie. Just a little favor I'm needing. If you're willing."

Opal needing a favor? From me? Now I really was worried. "Sure."

I led the way up the stairs and into the office. It concerned me when she closed the door behind her. She wasn't taking any chances. That most likely meant that this little meeting had to do with me being a Light Witch.

"What were you needing, Aunt Opal? You know I'll help you if I can."

Opal didn't answer immediately. She was staring intently at the door. "Is Liz visible all the time?"

I shrugged. "I really can't answer that. I'm afraid the whole ghost thing is still pretty new to me." I hesitated. "But it wouldn't surprise me if she could go invisible if she wanted to. I probably should ask her that."

In fact, I'd definitely be asking her that now that the thought was firmly in my mind. Opie and I didn't need an invisible audience in the bedroom. Not that I think Liz would abuse our privacy like that. Still, it was something that would be good to know.

"Yes, well. Do you think it's safe to talk here about... things? Or should we go to the farmhouse?"

I took a deep breath and thought about it. "According to the Goddess, we can trust Patricia. And we do know a pretty big secret of hers. What's the worst that could happen? Do you really think now that she knows me, she'd still turn me in?"

"Patricia is a very by the book young witch. I think that matter might still be up for debate. She might see it as a for your own good kind of thing."

Yeah, like turning me in would be a good thing for me. Or my family.

"I don't like to think this way, but like I said, we know a big secret about her too, don't we? One she wouldn't want to get out?"

Opal still didn't look too sure, but at least she sat down. "If you think it's okay, then we can do this here."

She opened up the bag she'd brought up with her and took out two large crystals. I looked them over closely. They appeared to be the round type that many fortune tellers used to divine the future. Or at least convince the gullible that they were divining the future. I'm still not certain that kind of thing can be done with any kind of true accuracy.

"What are those for?"

She just looked at me. "If you think about our recent conversation downstairs, I think you'll know the reason I brought them."

I looked at them even closer and swallowed. "You want me to fill them with my magic?"

"Only if you are willing. It is odd that Gaston is the one that came up with the magic draining theory, when I have in my possession the tools to do the exact same thing with you."

Another gulp. "You want to drain my magic?" My voice kind of broke on the last few words.

Opal laughed. "Of course not. Well, not drain so much as pull from it. Remember when you helped me with some of the larger spells when you first got your power?"

I nodded.

"Well, this would be like that. Only you wouldn't have to take time out of your day to come to the farmhouse. You could keep one crystal ball here, and I would take the other with me. I've made sure that they are connected well. If you have magic to spare, you can push it into your crystal, kind of like making a deposit at a bank. Then I can make a withdrawal on my end when I need it."

I was quiet for a minute. Not because of what she was asking me to do. I had no problem with that at all. Not one tiny bit. I was quiet because of why she might be asking me to do it.

"Gaston isn't the only one whose magic is failing, is he?" It came out as almost a whisper.

"He is not." Her face flushed, and she looked

away, not meeting my eyes. "I had thought the waning power was simply an indication of the trouble the Goddess is having keeping things together. That perhaps she wasn't having the time to deliver her blessings to us as regularly as she had in the past. Now, I am thinking there is something far more sinister going on."

"Yeah, me too. Gaston made a pretty good case for that, didn't he?"

"Indeed. Are you willing to do this?"

I took another minute. "You should know I am. But I have a question for you first."

Opal's brows drew together as she looked at me. "You know I won't use the magic for evil."

"Of course, I know that! My question was whether or not you had access to more of those crystal balls." I hesitated. "And maybe slightly smaller ones that could be carried around."

Opal broke out in a large smile. "Oh, I do like the way you think, Amie."

Chapter 18

I didn't even tell the others what I had planned. I was half afraid they would try to talk me out of it. If what we thought was going on was really happening, then I was walking straight into the lion's den, so to speak. But it was something that had to be done. Of all of us, I was the logical one for a couple of reasons.

First of all, the council still thought of me as a useless witch. Therefore, they didn't think they had anything to fear from me. How could a witch with no magic possibly be a threat to them?

Second of all, I could defend myself if needed. Oh, sure, the rest of my family could defend themselves too. But I would be much more effective at it then pretty much all of them combined. Hey, I didn't ask for this kind of power, but I'd sure as heck use it to protect my family if need be. Not to mention protecting the whole magic community at large, and quite possibly the entire world.

Not that there was any kind of pressure or anything. Geesh. I hoped the Goddess hadn't put her faith into the wrong witch. I wasn't one that liked the feeling of facing nearly insurmountable odds. Usually, I backed away from challenges unless I was forced to face them. What can I say? I was a laid-back kind of witch. Live and let live.

Too bad we weren't all that way. We wouldn't be in this mess to begin with.

It had taken me half the night to come up with a plan. Part of that time was researching the current librarian, Rebecca Kimble. Rebecca had been at the council library's helm for almost a full decade. Ever since she retired from the large Oak Hill Library. She was good at what she did, so she had been immediately recruited. She'd accepted with grace. Come to find out, the retirement hadn't been her idea.

While she was a witch, she wasn't an elemental. That rather surprised me. At least it surprised me until I thought of Lily. Lily wasn't an elemental either. But I still wouldn't want to cross her in a battle of magic. I don't think Lily would fight fair. Or pull her punches, for that matter. In a word, Lily was scary, even without an elemental power behind her. I had no reason to believe that Rebecca couldn't be the same.

My biggest problem was not knowing how to approach her. Until we could prove she wasn't in on this, we had to assume she was. That made her very, very dangerous.

That's when the self-doubt started kicking in. Maybe I wasn't the witch for this after all. I wasn't exactly known for my subtlety.

Too late for those kinds of thoughts now, though, as the huge wooden doors were already right in front of me.

I'd left Patricia in Ruby's care after applying a little magic to boost the healing spell for her. The two of them were actually starting to bond a little. Patricia seemed to like Ruby's new look. And Ruby was just grateful for someone to appreciate the effort she'd put into it. I just hoped she didn't decide to make Patricia one of the bounty hunting team. We were full up, as it were. We didn't need any more hunters.

Why was I thinking of this now? Because I was just being me and putting off the inevitable act of walking through those intimidating doors.

I took a deep breath and tried to do just that. My hand touched the doorknob, and the knob started to glow. What it didn't do was turn.

After a few seconds, a panel of the door shimmered and disappeared, replaced with a wooden replica of Rebecca's face.

"To what end do you request entry to the Council Library?"

I stared into the fake eyes and replied, "To seek knowledge."

The wooden eyes didn't blink. It was rather unnerving.

"To what end do you seek knowledge?"

I swallowed and opened my heart and mind before answering. The one thing I didn't open was my magic. That, I couldn't afford to do. Not here. "To better myself and become a more productive member of the society of witches and community in general."

The face gave a brief nod. "So be it." And the knob turned in my hand.

I'd passed the first test. The second waited for me just inside the door.

The doors opened into a small entryway with no apparent way out. The room was nothing more than four tall and bare walls. Yes, even the doors behind me had disappeared, replaced with nothing but a bare wooden wall.

I stood still, waiting. Not that I had a choice. But I'd admit freely that all of this was bloody well intimidating. I could see why I'd never been here before. No simple library card for this place. It wanted a piece of your soul.

A chill passed over my body. I'd always loved

libraries. They were some of my very favorite places on earth. This one, however, was seriously creeping me out.

"What do you want?"

The voice came out of nowhere and everywhere all at the same time. No face this time, though, just the voice. Luckily, it was a more human-sounding voice than that of the doors.

With a sense of deja vu, I repeated, "To seek knowledge."

"Cut the crap," the female voice said. I think I kind of liked her. "What do you want?"

"To talk to the librarian and do some research. I had an odd thing happen with my familiar."

"Are you Amethyst Ravenswind?" Was it just me, or did the voice seem to hold the tiniest bit of interest now?

"I am. Daughter of Sapphire and niece of Opal Ravenswind."

"Enter." There was a pause as nothing happened. "But wipe your feet first."

I smiled and did as instructed. As soon as the soles of my shoes were considered clean enough, one entire wall shimmered and vanished. What its disappearance revealed was everything I'd expected and so much more. A library and museum all in one. My fingers itched to touch some of the volumes of books, each I was sure holding some magical spell that could save the world. Or destroy it.

Looking into the cavernous space, I finally realized why the security was so very tight. This place held infinite wisdom and knowledge. In a simpler term, it was dangerous. In the wrong hands, very, very dangerous.

What did that say about the person in charge of it? I'd have to watch my step around her for sure. With all this wealth of knowledge at her very fingertips, she could be very, very dangerous in her own right.

"I'm over here," the voice called out. I looked toward it and finally saw the librarian. She was sitting calmly at a huge desk, piled high with paperwork and books of all shapes and sizes. "What it is you wish to talk to me about? I do so hope you don't start with the weather or other small talk. My time is too valuable to waste on trivial things, you know."

"I totally agree." Then I hesitated. Something was really bothering me. The hair at the back of my neck was standing on end. Not in a magical kind of way. Rather, a someone is watching us kind of way. Creepy in the extreme.

I made my way to the desk, which was a considerable distance away. Once I was standing before her, I whispered. "I do not think we are alone."

Her eyes widened slightly as one eyebrow slowly rose. "Indeed. And what makes you think this?"

Before I could respond, the air shimmered to the side of her and none other than Lily Hilton, hedgewitch extraordinaire, appeared. She was sitting in a chair just behind and to the side of the librarian. I might have let out a slight gasp. Or maybe not so slight of a one.

Lily smiled at me, but her words were for the librarian. "I told you she would sense me here."

The librarian grunted. "Well, no one else ever has." Her sharp eyes raked over me. "I thought this one had limited magical abilities?"

I was getting rather annoyed at being talked about as if I wasn't standing right in front of them.

"My magical abilities might be limited." After all, everyone has their limits, rights? "But there is nothing at all wrong with my intuition."

Another grunt and a slight nod. "Very well. You've found us out. I would deeply appreciate it if you would keep the fact I have a visitor to yourself."

I looked at Lily and then back at her. "Why?" I wasn't getting it. The library was open, within limits, to witches in need of research. Surely the council wasn't so bigoted that they limited that access to only the elementals when they had recruited a hedgewitch as their librarian.

The two older women shared a long look. "I think I would prefer it if we didn't have to answer that. Some things aren't for public knowledge. My visitor and her reasons for being here are two of them. Are you willing to keep our little secret?"

Looking into her strict and unwavering eyes, I had to wonder what she would do if I answered no. Not that I would ever do that. I liked Lily a lot and couldn't bring myself to believe that her visit here had anything to do with hatching evil plans. Lily might not live the cleanest of lives, but she wasn't evil. Just a little misguided in some things. But she was getting better even at that.

"No one shall hear of it from me." I paused. Perhaps I could use this to my advantage. "But, if I may ask, does that courtesy extend both ways?"

Her eyes narrowed, and she stared at me for a long moment. Lily, for her part, was silent. This was between me and the librarian.

"That would depend on what your secret was, now wouldn't it?"

"But therein lies the problem, doesn't it? I don't wish to reveal my secret to you any more than you do to me."

The stare continued. "Then we may have a bit of a problem. I can't agree to such a blanket agreement."

"Oh yes, you can, Becky." Lily finally spoke. "I know Amie quite well, and she hasn't broken my trust yet. In fact, I owe her a great deal for that. She's good through and through, just like the rest of her family."

The librarian arched an eyebrow at her. "Well, you would think that, wouldn't you? After all, you're practically family yourself. Isn't it possible that you are seeing her through rose-colored glasses?"

And they were back to talking as if I wasn't there. This was growing old. Time to take a huge risk. I looked at Lily. I trusted her judgment of people better than my own. After all, I'd been wrong a lot in my life.

"Lily, can I fully trust the librarian? Is she good through and through as well?"

They both looked at me, startled. "Well, of course, she is," Lily said. "Do you really think she would be in this position if she wasn't?"

I hesitated. That was the problem in a nutshell. Someone in a high-ranking position was doing something nefarious. To my mind, that made her current position a liability rather than an asset. I took a deep breath and made the plunge. "Unfortunately, someone high up is up to no good." My eyes went to the librarian, who was now staring at me with increased interest. "I'd like to know I can trust her."

The librarian tore her eyes away from mine with reluctance and looked to Lily. I could tell there was something that she wanted to ask her. But I could also tell that she didn't want to do so in my presence.

Lily nodded to her friend. That's what I firmly believed the two of them to be. Fast friends. "I would trust Rebecca Kimble, Librarian of the Council Library with my life. She is good through and through."

I swallowed down my worry. But I had one more question before revealing my secret. "Would you trust her with Merlin's life?" Sometimes we value our loved ones even more than ourselves.

The librarian chuckled. "I'd like to hear the answer to that one myself, Lily."

Then Lily did something that I would never in a

million years have expected her to do. She stuck her tongue out at the librarian. Then she turned to me. "Not as much as I would trust myself, but second only to myself and your family, yes I would trust her with even my precious Merlin's life. Does that answer your question?" Then her voice grew softer. "You really can trust her, Amie. She's a good one."

That was all I needed to know. I might not know the librarian yet, but I knew Lily.

I just really hoped she was right about this.

Our lives and the world at large might just rest on Lily's judgment call.

Chapter 19

The librarian gave me a hard stare. "So, if you're satisfied that I can be trusted, would you mind telling us what your visit is really about?" She hesitated for a split second, then continued. "But keep in mind I do want the first-hand story of you and your first familiar as well."

I looked at Lily and nodded. I was really hoping that she hadn't shared all the particulars with her friend as to that story. Like me being a Light Witch. Although, if she had, then the librarian might be on our side after all. I mean, I wasn't in a magic draining box, was I?

"Sure thing, but it might have to wait. I'm kind of on an important mission." My mind was racing, trying to come up with a new plan now that my old one had flown out the window. Telling the truth was one thing, but telling the whole truth was out of the question. Yes, we Ravenswinds have had personal conversations with the Goddess, but I'm not at all sure that other, non-family member witches, would be willing to accept that as fact.

It wasn't a widely done thing. The Goddess was far too busy of an entity to make personal house calls on a regular basis. She kind of figured we could use her blessings to do what needed to be done. Most of the time, anyway. This time was very different. There was simply too much at stake.

"I understand that the library keeps samples of all the council member's magic. I wanted to see them."

That got a reaction. The librarian sat up even straighter and her face set to a stony expression. "And why would you want to do that?"

In for a penny, in for a pound, my Grand used to say. "Because I think they are being used in a bad way."

Lily stood up and placed her hand on her friend's shoulder. "The trust thing can go both ways, Becky. Remember, Amie and her family could be trusted with Merlin's life too."

The librarian still hesitated, but finally, she gave a short nod. "I do hope you are right on this, Lily. The more people we let in on this, the greater the danger that the ones involved will learn of it."

I totally agreed on that one, and I wanted them to know that. "My family and I are personally invested in getting to the bottom of this. In a way I can't really explain. I can say that we are working with Patricia Bluespring, and with the guidance of the Goddess."

If I'd expected some kind of debate on that last part, I'd have been disappointed. She took my words at face value. "I've always known you Ravenswinds were personal favorites of the Goddess. You don't get that much power in one family without that being the case." She paused. "So be it. On one condition. If we tell you what we know, you do the same. Tit for tat and all that."

Now it was my turn to hesitate. "I will tell you all I can about the magic stored here and what we know of it. I'm afraid it isn't much. That's kind of why I'm here, after all."

She nodded. "Well, don't expect to get a wealth of knowledge from us on it, either. We're pretty much in the dark as well." Then she stood and held out her hand. "Long past the proper time, but I'm Rebecca Kimble, by the way." She paused as we shook hands. "I think if we are going to be working together, you might be able to call me Becky. In private, though. I have a reputation as a hard-nosed witch, and I'd kind of like to keep it. Makes it easier to keep the order around here."

I could understand that. Kind of reminded me of my Aunt Opal, actually. I'd grown up thinking she was the hardest-nosed witch of all time. But when Nancy had shown up, she had softened. Then when baby Pearl was born, well, she wasn't exactly a pushover now, but she wasn't nearly as unapproachable as she had been. So yeah, I got the whole keeping order thing.

Truthfully, I was starting to like Becky. More importantly, or more dangerously, I was beginning to trust her. Trust can be a dangerous thing. Especially when the keeper of said trust stepped away from her desk, and I noticed her footwear. I'd gotten pretty familiar with the whole Doctor Scholls line of footwear in the past two days. And that's what she was wearing.

She must have caught me staring at her feet. "What?"

I coughed to buy myself some time. Finally, I asked, as nonchalantly as I could, "What kind of shoes are those?" I don't think my nonchalance thing worked very well, though, because there was a definite squeak in my voice there at the end.

She looked at Lily, who shrugged. "Don't have a clue what it's about, Becky."

Becky turned back to me. "They're Doctor Scholls. A member of the council swears by them and got me hooked on them. When you stand on your feet a lot during the day, a good pair of sensible shoes can help more than you think. I think he's got half the council wearing them now."

I closed my eyes for a second, relief pouring in. "Would that 'he' happen to be Gaston Crowe?"

She arched an eyebrow at me and nodded. "That

would indeed be the he to whom I was referring. Now would you kindly tell me what this is all about? Somehow, I don't think you are a connoisseur of shoes."

Swallowing, I considered my options. I kind of had to let her in on the whole magic draining thing as she was my only access to the magical sample room. The other investigation? Not so much. Besides, it involved Patricia and was more her story to tell than mine. Better to play it safe.

"Not a connoisseur, no. But I've recently spent a little time with Gaston, and I thought they looked familiar." I tried on a half-hearted shrug. "Kind of startled me to see you wearing basically the same shoes. That's all."

I felt kind of bad about the that's all. Up to that point, I'd been telling nothing but the truth. But once out of your mouth, you can't take words back. Even if you wish you could.

She frowned at me but left it at that. "Well, back to the matter at hand, then. The magical sample room is upstairs." Reaching down, she pushed a button on the desk, then took a small broach out of a drawer and pinned it to her lapel.

"That's the portable intercom system," Lily explained. "Basically, the library is locked down now. No one can get in without Becky's approval. She can give it through the intercom if need be."

I had to ask. "Do you really mean no one? Not even the council leaders?"

Two sharp pairs of eyes stared at me. "Why would you ask that?"

Another half-hearted shrug. "It could be important to know whether or not someone could interrupt us or hear our conversations. As the leaders of the council and this being the council library..." I let my words trail off. I wasn't about to give her everything I knew until I'd gotten at least something from her.

Her eyes narrowed even further as she stared at me for a minute in silence. "Crystal Waters and Tabitha Greenfield have twenty-four-hour access to the library and all it holds. Even I cannot keep them out." She paused. "Do you believe that could be a problem?"

"At this point, I don't know enough to say. I just don't want to run the risk of us being interrupted or spied upon. This is more important than you might now know."

She looked back at Lily and then nodded. "Very well." Then she reached down and pushed a couple of more buttons on the desk's control panel. "I just set the cowbell alarm and turned up the volume. If anyone, and I do mean anyone, comes in, we will know it instantly."

"Cowbell alarm?"

Lily grinned at me. "Call us old-fashioned if you will, but nothing says you've got company quite like a cowbell hanging on a door."

Ah.

Becky started walking toward a large and very ornate circular staircase, and I followed. Lily followed after me. I felt that I was personally being escorted with a guard in front and behind. It wasn't all that great of a feeling.

The upstairs had a wide balcony edged with a decorative safety railing. Standing at the railing, one could see most of the library below. At least the part that wasn't under the second floor. The balcony space was huge and filled with magical artifacts in glowing glass cases. I reached out to touch a particularly beautiful one, and Lily stopped me.

"Beauty isn't always something to be revered. That little gem has started wars."

I drew my hand back and took a closer look at some of the items now surrounding me. "These items are all dangerous, aren't they?"

"They are," Becky said. "And before you ask why they aren't under lock and key, rest assured that they are. This library is, in my estimation, one of the most secure facilities on the face of the planet. And that glow you see around each case is more than just a lock. If any of these cases are broken or opened, let's just say that things would get interesting very quickly."

I swallowed and nodded. What does it say about a hedgewitch that is given power over a display such as this one? That she isn't a witch to be messed with, for one.

Two small doors led off from the cavernous balcony museum, but Becky didn't head towards either of them. Instead, she walked over to stand under a large ceiling fan, which I noticed wasn't running. Other fans were working to keep the air circulating in this massive space, but this one wasn't spinning. Once Lily and I joined her under the lamp, she tugged twice on what I would have thought was the on and off cord.

"Step back a step," Becky said.

Even as we complied, the fan blades lowered into the room, stopping just inches from the floor. I looked up at the dark hole it left in the ceiling. I was guessing that was where the magic samples were, but how on earth did we get up there?

Then I noticed that both Becky and Lily had each stepped onto one of the three fan blades. "Step up, if you want to come," Becky said.

I did. As soon as my weight hit the blade, we started moving up. The unexpected motion almost threw me off balance, but Becky and Lily had been ready for that. A hand came to either side of me to steady my position.

The ride up was short, but it had my brain whirling like one of the working fans now below us. If items of extreme power were just left out in the open within this very secure building, then why so much secrecy for this room?

What exactly was I heading up into?

156

Chapter 20

The room was dark. Pitch black, in fact. "Stay where you are," Becky warned. "Don't step from the blade until you are given leave."

Given leave? By whom?

Then the darkness ebbed, and a single flame's width of light came into view. "Speak the password that is your soul." The flame danced around the words as they were spoken. It wasn't a voice, nothing that could be explained quite that easily.

Becky's voice came from the darkness. "Knowledge."

I felt a slight movement beneath me as Becky stepped from the blade. What the heck? The password that is your soul? What did that even mean?

Then Lily's soft voice spoke. "Merlin."

I was sensing a pattern. Not knowing what would happen if I guessed wrong, though, was rather worrisome. But from what I gathered about lifelong librarians, knowledge was pretty much what filled their hearts. And I knew for a fact that Lily loved Merlin more than life itself.

So what was my soul's password? Opie? I loved him dearly, but I also loved my parents and my cousin. The Goddess had given me a destiny not of my choosing, but that was a matter more of duty than heart and soul.

The small dancing flame floated up to mere inches before my nose. I had to force myself not to swat it away. Didn't the thing recognize a gal who needed to think?

Finally, I took a deep breath and spoke the one thing that always brought my soul peace. It brought a lot of pain along with it sometimes, but that happened.

"Family."

If I didn't know any better, I'd have sworn the little flame nodded in agreement. Right before it disappeared.

"Lights on," Becky called out.

Instantly we were bathed in clear, clean white light. I looked at my feet. They were still firmly planted on the blade. No one had said that I could step off yet. I assumed that I'd passed the test, but I wasn't willing to take any chances.

"You can join us now, Amie," Lily said calmly. "You did well. I thought family might be your password, but I simply wasn't sure. It could have been... well, something else entirely."

I swallowed. Yeah, I'd had that thought myself. "Just out of curiosity, what would have happened if I had given the wrong password?"

"You would have been dropped into a vat of boiling oil until your flesh disappeared and nothing was left but a bubbling dab of goo," Becky said, her face deadpan.

I stared at her in horror. "What?"

Lily chuckled. "Come on, Amie, do you see any vats of boiling oil around?"

I glanced around me for the first time, really taking in my current surroundings. There were a number of glowing crystals, but no. There was no vat of boiling oil. "You have a very weird sense of humor, Becky, but you still didn't answer my question."

She smirked at me. "Your feet would have remained glued onto the blade, and you would have been returned to the floor beneath this one. You would have remained there, too, until I spoke the freeing word." She hesitated. "Of course, should you try three times without speaking the right word, then.... well, let's just say things get more serious."

I swallowed. Somehow, I didn't doubt her words one bit. And even though I had been the one to ask the question, I didn't really think I wanted the answer to that one.

"I would like your initial impression of the sample library, if you would be so kind as to give it."

Nodding, I looked around at the glowing displays. They weren't a consistent color, but I didn't expect them to be. Each witch's magic was a slightly different shade from any other. It was part of why our magic was so traceable back to us. A small part, but still a part.

The first thing I noticed was that there were far more than just thirteen crystals. Without taking a detailed count, I'd say there were at least three times that amount, and maybe more. The second thing I noticed was that my hair was floating on its own accord. That was super odd because my hair only floated when magic was passing through it. And I wasn't using any at the time.

That's when I realized that my skin was fairly itching with magic. Not my magic. Magic from all the surrounding crystals.

My heart filled with dread. I think I could safely say at this point that Gaston's theory was spot on. Someone was draining witches' powers through their sample crystals.

Turning to Becky, I looked her directly in the eyes. "My initial impression? We have a very serious problem."

"No crap, Sherlock," Lily said. "We noticed a few days ago that the magic was leaking from the samples. We don't know why, or how to stop it."

I had to ask one more time. "You'd really trust Becky with Merlin's life?"

"What the dickens is it that you know that we don't?" Becky's tone let me know that there would be no dancing around this one. I just really hoped that Lily was right about her. It would take someone with unfettered access to this room to be able to pull this off.

Someone just like Rebecca Kimble.

***

In the end, it all boiled down to my trust in Lily. She'd helped my family in some pretty rough times, and even though she had some flaws, didn't everyone? Luckily, the Goddess loves us even when we aren't perfect. Or even very far from it.

I told them the bare bones of what we suspected, and by the light in Becky's eyes, I could tell that I'd pretty much just confirmed her own suspicions. At this point, it was time to get the entire team together and make a plan.

We had the main suspects, at least to the whole witches' council investigation, narrowed down to two. Well, two if you took into account the trust Lily had in Becky. Which I did. Totally.

Okay, mostly. Let's just say I don't give my trust as easily as I used to. I've changed a bit in that regard over the past several months. And with good reason, too.

Everyone came to our house, not because we had the largest space available to seat everyone—Mom and Archie had us beat hands down there—but because that way Patricia could be included. Liz wasn't an issue. First of all, she was dead, but second of all, this was witch business. And while she was a werewolf, and family, that's where her similarity to Patricia ended. She wasn't a witch. More importantly, she'd never been a witch when she was alive either.

Mom thought ahead and brought some fold-up chairs to help with the seating issues, and we all met in my front living room. And I mean everyone. All of my family, to include the Minehearts, Lily, Becky, and Patricia. Not to mention the two little Goddess kitties. To see their expressions, they were the ones running the show.

When I stopped to think about it, they were probably right at that. Not even my family ranks above the Goddess. She's kind of the top of the food chain.

The only one missing was Opie. He'd opted out. I could totally understand that. I was hoping that he was taking the time to start packing up his apartment to move in here. But a gal can't be pushy and actually suggest that, now can she?

Lily and Becky arrived last, and I could tell that Becky wasn't happy to see so many people gathered in the room. Her eyes sought out mine.

"Are you absolutely sure this is wise?"

I nodded. "If we are right, then the other side has a heck of a lot of stored and available magic at their disposal. That being said, we will need all the help we can get." I motioned to my family. "I personally vouch for each and every one here." Well, except for her, but I thought that much was implied.

We all took seats, Arc, Ruby, and I opted to use our meditation pillows on the floor rather than a folding chair. The nicer furniture was reserved for the older witches and our guests.

Finally, when everyone had settled in, I started.

"So, everyone here knows what this is about, and what we suspect is happening. To lay it on the line, someone high up in the council is using the magic samples provided by the council members to steal their magic." I nodded to Becky. "Bec..., I mean Ms. Kimble here is the librarian of the council. She had at first thought the magic was leaking from the samples, but unfortunately that isn't the case. If it were, the crystals would be empty by now, but they are not. They are being used as conduits to the member's magic."

I looked over at Becky. "I have a quick question, though, before we start coming up with a plan. There were a lot more than thirteen crystal globes in that room. Who do they belong to?"

Her lips formed a thin line. "It's rather controversial."

I arched an eyebrow and waited. So did everyone else.

Finally, she got the hint that we weren't budging. We couldn't afford for there to be secrets among us. We needed to be open and willing to share everything if we would have any hope of stopping whatever the heck it was that was happening.

"Fine. But you didn't hear it from me." She took a deep breath. "The witches' council as we know it isn't really all that old. Only a few generations, and once you are on the council, well, it's kind of a life-long thing. Only, it really isn't. Life-long, I mean. It's longer than that."

Every eye was staring at her. Hard. Opal was the one to speak first.

"Are you saying that you still have access to past council members and their magic?" Her voice rose in disbelief. "My mother's magic?"

Rebecca shifted in her chair. With anyone else, it might be called a squirm. "Access to them, no." She hesitated. "Access to their magic, yes."

Opal met my eyes. This was so not good. Gran was a very powerful witch.

"Are you saying you have access to a sample of her magic? As in only a small amount?" I held my breath, hoping that was the case.

Rebecca shook her head. "I wish that were the case. I'd always thought it was, until recent events. But as witches, we aren't the source of our magic." She waved her hand around her. "It comes from the earth and the sky, and for some of you, the very elements of nature. When a witch dies, the magic lives on. Until today, I had thought the magic stored in the library's attic was a static and unchanging thing. Now I know differently. The magic is flowing... and refilling the globes continuously. All of them."

Crapsnackles. I was right. This was so very, very bad.

The bottom line was that not only did the bad guys have access to all the council members' magic, they also had access to the magic of some of the most powerful witches of the past century or more. To include my Gran.

It might sound funny, but that really ticked me off. The thought that someone could use my Gran's magic for evil when she wasn't even around anymore to help stop them? It was so not right.

We had to stop this. And just like that, it became more than a mission from the Goddess.

It became personal.

Chapter 21

Our plan was a simple one. Draw the bad guys out and then deal with them.

To do that, we had to find a way to stop the magic from flowing from those magical holding orbs. That was a job for Opal, Mom, Lily, and Becky.

My job? Well, I like to think it was just as important. When we finally came face to face with the ones responsible for this, and I had absolutely no doubt that there was more than one involved, we would be facing a tremendous amount of power.

That was a very scary proposition. Actually, it was a terrifying proposition. One that would stop me in my tracks if I'd been doing this alone. Or if the stakes weren't as high as they were.

Bottom line, we needed stored power too. Something we could draw on in the time of battle. That was my job.

Ruby, Arc, and the others were all working on this too. Now that we knew that we could store power for later use, well, it was just a smart thing to do. Our magic isn't endless. Or perhaps it is. But our ability to pull it definitely wasn't. Magic had to have time to regenerate.

The bad guys had found a way to bypass that. The good news was that now we knew their little secret and could use the bypass too.

Opal had a fair amount of crystal items at her shop, and I went online and ordered more. All that my limited budget would allow. Mom and Dad chipped in and brought over a whole box of crystal beaded bracelets.

A great idea that. Wearable magic.

I spent my time filling the crystals. Having access to more magical power than the others, the biggest chunk of this had to be done by me. Not that I minded. It felt great being able to do something that might make a difference in the end.

Within three days, all the crystals were filled, and the spells to allow us to access them were done. Becky had been the one to finally crack the code as to how to stop the magic flow from the orbs too. That surprised me. I'd figured it would be Opal.

I really hoped she wasn't slipping.

***

We stopped the magic flow first thing the following morning. With the library being open and witches somewhat coming and going, we didn't think the bad guys would take the risk of a daylight visit.

That didn't mean we weren't prepared for it. Let's just say my family decided that now was a good time to do a bit of research at the library.

That night, we would all be there. Hidden within the walls of the massive space.

And when I say hidden, I meant it.

Merlin called on his friend Jack, the magical burglar, to cast stealth spells on all of us. We didn't want to be seen entering the library and not exiting. No sense in giving the evil witches advance notice of trouble.

But for the day, it was just Opal, Ruby, and me.

I had kind of hoped that the evil ones would make a visit during the day, so I was watching all the ones that came and went. With special attention to any who climbed that circular staircase.

The library was extra busy that day, which had me worried. According to Becky, a normal day saw maybe a dozen witches. Today, we had three times that.

I hoped that didn't portend really bad things. Like the fact that this just might be bigger than we had originally thought.

Two of those visitors were our main suspects: Tabitha Greenfield and Crystal Waters. Both of them went up the stairs too. But the ceiling fan stayed in place the whole time.

Not wanting to make them nervous by following them, we used a hidden camera. Not magical, I know, but sometimes old school technology has its place. This was one of them.

They seemed more interested in a particular artifact. I'd have to remember to ask Becky more about it later. If it drew that much interest from them, it had to be something special.

Unless, of course, their interest was only a decoy to get closer to the orbs above them. But they didn't even glance upward. They simply studied the object in the case and then came back downstairs and left.

I breathed a lot easier after that.

The rest of the day was pretty uneventful, and we used the time to catch up a bit as a family. It was a nice enough way to pass the time. It would have been nicer without the added stress, but you work with what you have.

Once the library closed, our other crew members arrived one by one. According to Jack, the stealth spell worked better that way. It was too hard to hide several people all at once.

The rest of us took turns leaving, getting spelled by Jack, and then returning. By a little after dark, we were as ready as we ever would be.

Which was a good thing, because it didn't take long for them to show up.

"It's Tabitha and Ginger!" Becky whispered.

Once again, we'd used hidden cameras to give us a bit of advance warning. It might be against the fire code, but there was only one real entrance to the library. According to Becky, the exiting wouldn't be a problem should the need arise. I was taking her word for it. Tonight, it came in handy as we didn't have to spread out to cover more than one entrance.

We were all right there when Tabitha Greenfield strode through the door.

Ginger, however, didn't. She stopped right at the threshold, her eyes wide.

"Tabitha, wait! Something's wrong!"

I wasn't sure at first what tipped her off, but somehow, she knew it was a trap. The same couldn't be said for Tabitha.

Tabitha turned to Ginger. "What are you talking about? Come on."

Ginger shook her head. "No. Something is wrong. You need to come back out."

The light bulb of my brain finally went off. We had placed wards on the library to keep anyone who wished harm to the Goddess out.

It spoke volumes that Tabitha was allowed in, but Ginger was not. Of all the council witches, I never would have thought it would turn out to be her. Live and learn.

Well, I hoped on the live part, anyway.

At Opal's word, we all stepped out, giving Tabitha a major start.

"What the...!"

"Good evening, Tabitha," Opal said with a grim smile. Then she turned to Ginger. For what it's worth, Ginger had my eyes on her the whole time. Once I figured out why she hadn't followed Tabitha in, there was no way I was letting her out of my sight. "Why don't you come in and join us, Ginger?"

"As the second in command of the witches' council, I demand to know what is going on! What are you all doing here after hours? The library is closed."

"And yet here are the two of you," Becky said, stepping up beside Opal. "But then only one of you managed to get inside. I find that very interesting. Must have something to do with the wards we put in place earlier tonight."

"Wards? What on earth are you talking about? The library has all the wards it needs. Exactly what ward did you place without the council's permission?"

"One that keeps out anyone who wishes harm to the Goddess and her followers," Opal said, eyes tight on Ginger.

"But, the library is for Her followers." Tabitha shook her head. "What is going on?"

"Why don't you ask Ginger? Or better yet, Ginger, why don't you come in and join us? Or can't you pass the threshold?" Becky asked.

The Ginger I'd known for years vanished. Oh, she still stood there, don't get me wrong. But the person I knew was no longer home in that body. Her eyes darkened to black, and a faint glow started up around her body.

Tabitha gasped and took a step back, closer to us, putting some distance between herself and the new Ginger.

"No matter. I'll make short work of your pitiful wards." Even Ginger's voice was... off. Deeper and darker, with a hint of gravel thrown in there too. She gave Tabitha an evil smile. "Why don't you join with the side of the winners, Tabby? Step out here with me."

Tabitha shook her head and took another step closer to Opal. Yeah, that's the one I'd rest my bets with too. Everyone knew the power of Opal Ravenswind.

"So be it. You know far too much to be allowed to continue." She raised a finger and pointed to Tabitha, but Opal was quicker than she was.

Raising her crystal bracelet, with all the stored power it contained, between them and Ginger, Opal stepped before Tabitha. The filled orbs back home were what we would use to draw power from. The bracelets? We'd set them up as a kind of force shield for protection.

The only question now was, would it be enough?

Chapter 22

It was, and it wasn't. All at the same time. While the bracelet's power most likely saved Opal and Tabitha's lives, Ginger's spell still took Opal down.

Hard.

Once I saw that she was still breathing—that, of course, had been my first priority—I turned to face Ginger with my own bracelet raised. I was hoping that she'd spent a whole lot of her power behind that blast and was feeling a little drained by now.

"I'm impressed," Ginger said dryly. "I'd heard how powerful your family is, but that spell should have disintegrated anyone it touched. That Opal Ravenswind still draws breath speaks to her power."

The non-Ginger voice was creeping me out. I didn't think we were dealing with an earthbound witch anymore.

"What have you done with Ginger?"

The voice laughed. "Oh, you are a smart one, aren't you? But you are right, of course. Ginger is no longer the one in charge of this human vessel. She is here, though, and safe enough. You might say we are sharing the space, but I fear it probably isn't very comfortable for her by this point." The face gave an evil smile. "I don't believe she fully comprehended my power."

Ginger's shared body shrugged. "Not that I care in the least, mind you. She gave her permission for me to enter, and that was all I needed. I'm in charge now."

Her eyes still lingered on Opal. "If only it had been that one, oh, the things I could have done... but no matter." The eyes raised to mine. "I don't suppose you all will see reason and join the greatness that is Ba'al?"

So that was who we were dealing with. Crapsnackles to infinity. This was so very, very bad.

"That isn't going to happen, Ba'al," I said between gritted teeth. I gritted them to keep them from chattering in terror.

That horrible, grating laughter came again. "Oh, that is rich. You think I am Ba'al? No, child, I am but a humble servant. Ba'al is so much more. But if you won't join us, then I do so hope you enjoy the next few minutes of your life. There won't be many of them."

I stood my ground. I could see out of the corner of my eyes that every one of us had our bracelets raised, and they were all glowing. The others had gone one step farther than I had. They were pouring power from the orbs back home into their shields.

Something I should have done, but it required concentration. I wasn't willing to break my will power battle with Ba'al's minion now to draw it. But then, I had power of my own.

"I believe you underestimate the Goddess and her followers," I said. "Perhaps you are the one who should consider a religious conversion."

The laughter swelled. "Oh, I think I like you. Too bad I won't be enjoying your company for long."

Without warning, the finger came up again and pointed directly at me. Instantly, my magic came to full force, and I let it flow into the bracelet. When the spell hit the crystals, they shattered. A few of the crystal splinters dug into the exposed skin of my arm.

Hopefully, I'd still be alive to deal with them later.

The main thing was, I was still standing. And unharmed.

Ginger's eyes widened. "That isn't possible. According to Ginger, you have no true magic. How?" Then the face set into apparent stone. "No matter. I can level this building, and all inside will perish. Magical bracelets or no."

I guessed that her stored magic must be running low. Otherwise, I think she would have followed up with another blast now that my force shield was down. Or possibly she had realized that each of us was wearing them, and knew her magic wasn't enough to take us all on.

"No!" Becky rushed to my side. "This library holds irreplaceable knowledge. You can't destroy it!"

I noted that she said nothing about our pitiful lives. Only the library. But then, as the librarian with a soul password of knowledge, I guess that only made sense.

I gave Ginger an evil smile of my own. "Don't worry, Rebecca, that's an empty threat if ever I heard one. You forget what the attic of this place holds. Their source of unending magic."

Becky swallowed and muttered under her breath. "I hope you're right on this one, Amie."

So did I.

Ginger's head tilted as her eyes narrowed at me. "Smart indeed. So what are we to do now? As you know, I cannot enter. Are you all going to cower inside under the false protection of your glorious Goddess? Or are you willing to come to me and have us finish this once and for all?"

I took a deep breath and swallowed. "I don't suppose you all would let me handle this?"

"Not happening," Mom said. "But I agree with

the settling this thing."

The others stepped forward too. We were all in agreement. We would finish this. Possessed and drawing power or not, Ginger was only one witch. There were a lot of us. We had numbers on our side.

I wish I could say that seemed to bother Ginger, but it didn't. She looked far too confident to make me happy.

She stepped back from the doorway to allow us all to exit. We stuck close to each other. It might have been smarter to spread out and widen her field to attack, but that wasn't our style.

We didn't want to lose a single member of the crew. Not one. We were kind of like the Musketeers in that respect. All for one and one for all.

I felt a lot better when I felt Opal's hand grasp my shoulder from behind. I'd have felt even better if I hadn't realized she was doing it to draw strength to stand. She was hurting. I wanted to send her a little healing magic, but I needed every ounce of power for the battle to come.

But then again, what was it we were fighting for? I sent her a trickle of healing. From her slight gasp and stronger grip, I took it that it helped.

"So, how do we do this?" Mom asked, taking over the leadership for once. It was a side of Mom I rarely saw. She was always following Opal's lead, not leading herself.

Ginger's smile widened. "Why now we fight, of course."

There was movement around her. The air shimmered with flashes of light and suddenly, she was no longer alone. A very quick count showed twelve other witches surrounding her. Not council witches, though. That was good.

What was really, really bad was the fact that

each and every one of them was glowing with unused power.

      This would not be pretty.

Chapter 23

"You didn't seriously think I came alone, did you?" She smiled at the witches now surrounding her. "This is my coven. As you can see, we are—how do you say it?—locked and loaded for battle. This won't take long. I do hope you have all made peace with your God and Goddess. You'll be joining them soon."

"And you didn't think we'd let the Ravenswinds take all the credit for bringing you down, now did you?" The air didn't shimmer this time. Gaston and the two witches with him simply stepped out from the dark shadows.

Well, I say witches, but I'm quite sure Gaston would say that they were Shamans. All of them. It was pretty easy to tell, as they were all wearing original American Indian headdresses. Striking, actually.

Gaston looked over my shoulder at Opal. "I hope you don't mind if we join the party?"

"Reinforcements are much appreciated, Gaston."

"Good."

My family might have stayed pretty tightly grouped for protection, but the Shamans didn't follow that plan of attack. They spread out and surrounded Ginger and her coven. The numbers were a lot more even now.

Still, Ginger didn't appear to be worried.

"Actually, I much appreciate your appearance, too, Gaston. The more of you Goddess lovers I can take out all at once, the better."

"We aren't here for the Goddess, One Who Used to be Ginger. We are here for the Great Spirit. Ba'al should take note that it isn't only the Goddess he has to fear."

Raspy laughter filled the surrounding area. "I'll be sure to let them know."

The glow around Ginger and her crew started to brighten. They were drawing even more power. They might not be able to pull from the orbs in the library's attic, but it was quickly apparent that they had stored up power somewhere else to draw on. It was time to nip that in the bud.

The only problem was that rule of three thing. If we struck the first blow, we'd be reaping the backlash for decades. But waiting for them to strike first didn't seem to be much of an option either. That first strike was likely to be one heck of a doozy.

"Whenever you're ready, Becky, but sooner would be better," Opal said tightly behind me.

"Don't you think I've been trying?" Becky asked. "I don't have the power to reverse the flow."

Opal grunted, her grasp on my shoulder tightening just a bit. Then she reached out and grasped Becky's shoulder with her other hand. "You do now. Do it."

Reverse the flow? Obviously, the older witches hadn't let us young witchlings in on the entire plan. It might have been nice if they had.

Ginger laughed again. "Don't strain yourself, Rebecca. Whatever feeble attempt you are trying will be fruitless against the power that is... What the devil?"

That last part came as the glow around her and her coven flickered. It was a brief flicker, but enough to make Ginger stumble forward an inch or two. Wild eyes stared at Becky. Was that fear I saw in their depths?

"Stop her! The librarian, all of you. Now!" Ginger shouted.

Yup, definitely fear. The entire coven moved as one, lifting their pointy little fingers at Becky. Yeah, that wasn't going to happen.

I'd gotten pretty good at defensive spells in my short term as a Light Witch. We'd know just how good very soon.

Concentrating, I opened the doors to my magical sources. Both of them. Air and Earth. Magic flooded my body. As it turns out, the magic is always there, just waiting for me to let it in. Other witches have to take time to draw it to them. I just have to open the door.

My hands flew up, and I let the protective spell loose. I wished that Gaston and his shamans were behind me, too, because that's the area I was protecting with all my might and power. Well, almost all of it. Just enough of it was going via Opal to Becky. Enough to make the glow around the evil coven dim and ebb even more by the second.

When the collective spells hit, they were massive. But my spell held. Barely. Another blast like that, and it would break through.

But another blast didn't come. I'm not sure if they had the magic left for another one. That's something we'll never know, because that was when Gaston and his shamans opened fire on Ginger and her coven.

Opened fire. Strange way to say it, actually. Especially as it wasn't bullets they were spraying Ginger and her gang with, but water. I thought for a minute that maybe they had lost their grip on reality. Was it holy water? Blessed by the Great Spirit himself? Would it work?

Then I smelled it. Salt. They were dousing them with saltwater.

The witches started shrieking, and the attack stopped.

There was a loud sound above us, and Becky fell to her knees. "It's done." Whether it was the result of Becky's magical reversal or the saltwater, the glow was gone.

"What have you done?" Ginger cried. "Witches, take them."

But her witches were on the ground in pain. The magic they'd been sending out to attack us had been forced back on them by the saltwater. I would have to remember that little trick for later. Maybe instead of a taser, when dealing with witches, I'd start carrying a squirt gun. It seemed to work really well.

"It's over, Ginger. You lost." Opal stepped forward.

I saw the slight limp as she did so. She'd been hurt worse than she'd let on. If there was any permanent damage, I'd personally see to it that Ba'al and his minions paid in kind. I know it's technically against the rules, but when it comes to my family, I can be a very vindictive witch.

"It will never be over! Ba'al will never be defeated."

"But Ba'al isn't in charge here now. The Goddess is. And luckily for you, Ginger, She is a lot more forgiving than your current god. She'll take you back if you just say the word."

Wild eyes darted back and forth, not meeting Opal's gaze. "She is mine, body and soul."

Opal shook her head, still moving forward. "You are wrong. I don't believe for an instant that Ginger knew what she was getting into when she let you in. Your lot speaks lies fluently, but truth isn't something you share, is it?"

Opal was within reach of Ginger now. I wasn't sure what her plan was, but I really hoped she knew what she was doing.

"All you have to do is the say the word," Opal repeated, not budging.

Ginger screamed and lunged for Opal. But she was ready for the move. At least, I think she was. They did both end up on the ground, so I couldn't be totally sure.

At this point, the magic had been spent, and it was just two women duking it out. Ginger was younger, and Opal was hurt. It really wasn't much of a contest.

The minion in Ginger didn't stand a chance. Within seconds of them hitting the earth, the rest of us were pulling them apart, or trying to. Opal was holding on tightly.

So was Ginger. Her head was resting on Opal's shoulder, and she was crying. "Yes," she said.

A red puff of what looked slightly like a smoky form with horns floated above her. "This isn't over. It will never be over." The voice was creepy as heck when it had a voice-box to go through. Now? It was even more disturbing.

Opal looked up at the floating smoke. "You're right. But it's over for Ginger." She nodded to the rest of Ginger's coven. "And I think it's over for them too."

The form let out a blood-curdling shriek of rage, and the smoke dissipated until there was nothing left but the cold night air.

"Let's get them inside," Becky said, reaching a hand down to Opal. "I think some of them need medical attention."

Opal nodded. "Yes. I think I could use a bit of that myself."

Chapter 24

That loud sound that we'd heard above us had been the shattering of the magical sample library. The orbs were destroyed. All of them.

Becky said they wouldn't be replaced, and I believed her. Now that we knew the danger and temptation they could bring about, it simply wasn't a good idea.

The only one I felt bad about losing was the one filled with Gran's magic. I would have like to have kept that. It had been nice knowing that a small part of her lived on. But then there was always Baby Pearl.

At least she lived on in name, if nothing else. Maybe that was enough.

Ginger and her coven had been turned over to the council, and Tabitha had resigned her position.

No, she hadn't had anything to do with Ba'al or his evil plan, but she had been the one to give him access to the orbs via Ginger. She'd been used by a friend she loved and trusted.

No one would have demanded her resignation, but she offered it anyway. Maybe it was for the best. We didn't really need someone second in command that made that bad of decisions.

Once Crystal and the council authorities showed up, we were pretty much done for the night. In every imaginable way. Exhaustion didn't even begin to cover it. At least this time I didn't faint. I have a feeling that my ability to handle magic was growing stronger.

Truthfully, that had me more than a little worried. Everyone should have limits. Even Light Witches.

Crystal hadn't been happy about being kept out of the loop in all of this. I could respect that, but what choice had we had? If the council has rot growing in it, isn't it only natural to assume it starts from the top and works its way down?

Opal would have some bridges to mend with her, but that was Opal's problem. Not mine, thank the Goddess. Right now, I didn't have the energy to give to another problem.

I had enough of my own already.

Like what would happen with the house, and where I would be living soon. I know that Opie would let me stay with him, but that tiny little apartment would not cut it for long.

It might have been the exhaustion, but by the time I got home, I just wanted an answer. I wanted to know if I'd be moving in the next month or less. So when I entered the house to find Patricia and Opie quietly sitting in the front room sipping tea, I broke.

"What are you doing about the house, Patty? I just can't take not knowing any longer. Do I have to find another place to live?"

She blinked a few times, leaning heavily back against the couch. "And hello to you, too, Amie. Nice work with Ginger and her coven, by the way." She grimaced. "Really wish I could have helped with that. I'm not used to being on the sidelines for things like that."

Yeah, well, neither was Opie. I could tell he was still more than a little ticked off about us leaving him behind. But the bottom line is that we both have dangerous jobs sometimes. We just had to learn to trust our partner's skills to get them through it.

Not to say that there hadn't been a massive argument about him staying home earlier in the evening. But the fact that no non-witches were allowed anywhere near the library, and the fact that the others backed me up helped me win that one. For once.

I plopped down beside Opie on the loveseat and snuggled in. I was afraid I would need his comfort when Patricia finally answered my question. I knew she'd get around to it, eventually. So, I waited.

Finally, she chuckled. "You are a stubborn one, aren't you? Well, lucky for you, Trevor and I spent our sidelined time tonight working out a possible solution to make us all happy."

I twisted my head to look up at Opie. "You been holding out on me?"

He smiled down at me and then kissed the top of my head. "I wanted a chance to work things out first. Getting your hopes up and then dashing them wasn't what I wanted to do."

"Okay, so what's the solution?"

"Well, first of all, you should know it was never the house and barn that I wanted. Oh, I love them, don't get me wrong, but for personal living space… well, you've seen my house. I like a smaller, more controllable space for actually living in."

A faint flare of hope sprang up in my heart. "Are you saying you don't want the place?"

She shook her head. "I said it wasn't the buildings that I wanted. The land the buildings sit on is another matter altogether." She took a sip of her tea, letting me stew on that for a bit before continuing. "You see, my pack is pretty spread out over a few counties. Part of that is a wolf territorial thing, but another part of that is being a Benandanti and spreading our protection to different villages."

Opie must have seen my slight confusion. In my current exhausted state, it wouldn't take much to throw me off tonight. "I'll tell you about that later. According to Patty here, one of the Benandanti's main purposes in life is to protect their village. Makes sense that you wouldn't need more than one in a town to do that. Especially as there are so few of them around these days."

Patricia nodded. "Exactly. But we still like to meet at least once a month to have a run and catch each other up." She looked around her. "This place is pretty much dead center of our combined territories. Equal distance for everyone, and thus perfect to hold our meetings."

"Plus, there's the whole private property versus public property thing. If you think about it, the wolves are taking a risk every time they meet at that park," Opie said.

I mulled that over and nodded. Okay, I guess I could see that. "So, I'll ask again. What's the solution?" I mean, the buildings were part of the land now. We couldn't very well give her one without the other, now could we?

Patricia smiled at Opie. "Well, your man here has done some major research. As it happens, there is a small piece of acreage near here that will be placed on the market for sale in the next few days. Ten acres, and with only one small hunter's cabin. The cabin has running water from a well and has a wind turbine and solar panels for electricity. An off the grid tiny home."

Opie's arms tightened around me in a hug. "It'll take work and money, but I took a close look at Patty's current house, and I'm pretty sure we could have it moved to the property. Shouldn't take much to switch the power from the cabin to it, or just add solar panels to her home."

I swallowed. This just might work. There was the issue of money, though. We'd been saving every penny we could, but this council investigation thing had taken a lot of time out of our working schedule.

"How much money?"

"Quite a bit, but not so much that I think it will be a problem. The owner seemed willing to work out a contract deal," Opie said. "And Patricia has said that she'll pay the expenses to have her home moved and set up, so all we're on for is the purchase of the land and cabin. And that will run about what you still owe for this place, so it will pretty much be a wash."

"You'll trade us that property for this one?" I was holding my breath.

"If we can get it to all work out, and I see no reason why it shouldn't, then yes. I'll trade even stevens." She grinned at me. "I love my home, actually, and the thought of being off the grid is nice too."

"Plus, you get double the acreage for your wolfy runs," Opie said.

Her grin brightened. "Yeah, that too."

A lot of tension flowed out of my body. Tension that I had begun to believe had made my body a permanent residence.

"That's good then." We'd make it work.

I even kind of liked the idea of having Patricia as a neighbor. I was starting to like her.

Chapter 25

Opie didn't wake me the next morning before he left for work. He must have known how much I needed my rest to recuperate from the last evening's activities. I only wished the person pounding on my front door had shown me the same courtesy.

Throwing on my soft and fuzzy robe, I stumbled out of our bedroom and down the stairs. Liz met me halfway. "It's that Indian guy. The shaman."

What the heck was Gaston Crowe doing at my home at this hour?

I pulled open the door and stared at him. At least he'd come alone this time.

"What?"

He took one look at me and his eyes widened drastically. Yeah, knock on someone's door at this hour in the morning, and you get what you get. Around here that was me with bed-head hair, droopy eyes, and a bad attitude.

It didn't take him long to recover. "We need to talk about what happened last night."

I frowned at him. "Shouldn't you be talking to the council? It's in their hands now."

"I really didn't think you'd want me to do that. This is about you."

Crapsnackles.

I knew I'd shown a lot of power last night, holding back the cumulative blast of an entire hyped-up on stored magic coven, but I'd really banked on everyone being so caught up in their own part of the action not to have noticed that. It seemed Gaston was a born multitasker.

"So, can I come in?"

I had a good reason for my hesitation. Actually, I had two. Liz and Patricia. I was starting to like Patricia, yes, but I wasn't sure I was up to being that open and honest with her. She was still a no-nonsense by the book type of witch.

"Let's go to the barn. I'll grab my key." I knew that Arc would have already left for work, so the only one we'd be disturbing was Ruby. If we were quiet enough, she'd probably never even know we were there.

Once inside, Gaston took a long look around and nodded. "Not so humble an abode as one would have thought from the outside."

He wasn't wrong.

"Please have a seat." I flopped down on the chair and left the couch for him. Normally I would wait for my guest to be seated, but my knees weren't really cooperating with me being upright right now. Too much rested on the next few minutes.

I was hoping the fact that Gaston hadn't shown up as part of a trinity of witches meant something.

After settling on the couch, he met my gaze. "As a shaman, and under the blessing of the Great Spirit, I have the ability to see magic." He took a deep breath. "Most of us have a single source of magic. Air, water, fire, or earth. That was not the case with you last night."

I could deny it, but what good would that do anyone? Destiny came and jumped on my lap. She must have followed us over. Either that, or she'd been having a sleepover with Yorkie Doodle. She did that sometimes.

According to Destiny, her sister was a little 'too much' for her.

Reaching down, I started petting her. The feel of her soft fur under my shaking fingers helped to calm me. Not much, but every little bit of calm I could muster was a good thing. "And if that is true, what does it mean going forward?"

"I am not turning you over to the council, if that is what you are asking."

The words didn't give me the relief I was looking for. "I sense a but in there."

He nodded. "Because there is indeed a major but in there. What you did last night was both controlled and necessary, not what I had been led to believe was possible for a Light Witch." He paused. "I am thinking that your Goddess gave you this ability to draw from multiple magic sources for a reason. And I don't believe that reason is so that you can become a magical battery for the council's use."

Good. I didn't think so either.

"And the but?"

Our eyes locked for a full minute before he answered. "I'll be watching you. Very closely. I will become a part of your life. Not every day, but I will keep very close tabs on you from here out. Cross the line of control, and I will do what needs to be done."

It was a very good thing that Gaston hadn't met me several months ago when I'd first found my power. He'd have had me locked up for sure. Control wasn't something that had come easily to me.

I nodded. I mean, what choice did I really have? Absolutely none.

"Good. Then we have an understanding." For the first time this morning, Gaston smiled at me. "I do have a private confession to make. It would appear that an alliance has been made between the Great Spirit and your Goddess."

My eyebrows shot up. "Oh?"

"Yes. I had a dream, and both of them played a major part in it. It would appear they are a team now. How long it will last, who knows? But for now,... well, I guess that extends down to us as well, doesn't it?"

I gave that some thought. Gaston had saved our bacon last night with the whole saltwater in the squirt gun blasters thing. I had to think an outside of the box thinker like that would be useful to have on my team.

"I believe it does." I paused for effect. "Might even go so far as to say it makes us... family, in a way."

His smile widened. "Family. I quite like the sound of that."

Yeah. So did I.

After all, family was my soul password for a reason. And not all family was blood.

***

When I got back to the house, I found Patricia already up and sitting on the couch munching a bowl of cereal. She was looking a lot better with each passing morning. She might even be able to handle the stairs for an honest to goodness shower today.

I knew how much little things like that meant to a woman. Hot running water was a very good thing.

"I'm sorry if Gaston's knocking woke you up."

She raised her eyebrows and looked up at me. "Gaston is here?"

Okay, so maybe that wasn't the case. "He was. I took him over to the barn. He just left." I couldn't think of a good reason for taking him over to Ruby's, so I just left it at that. Luckily, she didn't question it. Something else was on her mind.

"I see." She took another bite and munched

slowly. After she swallowed, she looked away. "Actually, it was my phone that woke me. Ginger called."

That got my attention. "They're letting her make calls?"

She nodded. "I guess they are giving her the chance to put her life in order. The council is putting her into magical prison. They are stripping her of her power."

If she expected me to be upset about that, she would be disappointed. I had liked Ginger, but the woman had come close to bringing about the end of the world as we knew it. That wasn't something that could just be swept under the carpet and forgotten because she said she was sorry.

"So, what did she have to say?"

Patricia lifted one shoulder, but she didn't meet my eyes. "She wanted to say she was sorry. It was her that took that shot. Well, it was Ba'al's minion, actually, but as he was in her body at the time…"

"Yeah, that's complicated." I hesitated, but curiosity won out. "Did she happen to say how she knew you were a werewolf?"

"Come to find out she didn't. Know I was a werewolf, I mean. Not until she was up in that tree and saw me change with her own two eyes. But I guess when an entity takes possession of a human body, the whole Goddess' rule thing goes out the window. Ba'al knew what I was, and that I was snooping into Ginger's business. That was enough for him to take a crack at me."

It was really hard to ask the next question, but I had to know. "Is she going to tell anyone?"

Patricia shook her head. "No. The whole conversation was a bit on the cryptic side, as there was someone right there in the room with her listening in, but she said I didn't have to worry about her anymore. I think my secret is safe with her." She paused. "And even if she told…"

I nodded. Who would believe her? It would be more likely that the council would believe her brief hosting stint with Ba'al's minion had driven her a bit batty.

Something still didn't quite seem wrapped up in my mind, though. I sat there for a few minutes trying to bring it into focus.

"You said the Benandanti split up to cover more territory, right?"

She nodded.

"Do you think the Luparii might do the same thing?"

"I guess it's possible. Why do you ask?"

I told her about the deputy at the park. "He seemed very interested in the news reports about the wolves in the park, and I'm not at all sure I believe that bit about the photography thing." I looked her in the eye. "And he had time to run your license plate, so he knows who you are. I'd watch my step, if I were you. He might not have been the one that took the shot, but…"

"He could still be Luparii."

"Yeah."

"Thanks for the head's up. I'll do some checking on him when I get the chance. Maybe go and ask him for coffee or something. Make him see me as a person. If he is Luparii, maybe that will help."

Maybe, but I wouldn't count on it.

"Well, if you need help with him—or anything else, for that matter—just say the word. Like it or not, you're part of the Ravenswind clan now. You know that, right?"

She tilted her head at me. "I am?"

"Yup. And for the record, so is Gaston. Our

family is growing pretty fast. I think it's kind of nice. One can never have enough family, can one?"

Patricia smiled at me. "As someone with no living family left that I know of, I'd have to agree." She hesitated. "Does that mean I'm an ongoing member of Team Destiny too?"

Team Destiny. It had a really nice ring to it.

"Absolutely." I paused. "That is, if you want to be. It isn't mandatory to the whole family thing."

She thought for a minute, then nodded. "I think I'd like being on the team too." She made a face. "Maybe I can be more useful next time."

"You were pretty useful this time too. But I am sorry that it meant you had to get shot to kick things into high gear. Don't do that next time, okay?"

Patricia snorted. "I'll bear that in mind."

I'm sure that the Goddess wasn't through with us yet. There would be more missions, though hopefully not ones with the dire consequences of this last one.

But that was for another day. Today, I would be a lazy slug. I could hear my bed calling from upstairs.

Unfortunately, I hadn't even made it two steps before Ruby came bursting through the front door, in full bounty hunter attire.

"Grab your taser, I just got a line on where Al Bork is hiding out!"

Oh, Goddess, here we go again.

###

Author's Update: Yes, this is the final book in the Accidental Familiar series. But don't despair! Amie and her crew will be back in the future in a whole new series spin-off: The Team Destiny Series.

But for now, Opal is demanding that her story be told. And who am I to deny Opal Ravenswind? Book 1 of the Witch Reborn Series goes live on Amazon June 12, 2020! Paperback version of Witch of a Godmother is already available!

That being said, if the Benandanti and Luparri caught your interest, you can read more about them in The Benandanti Series.

A Note From Belinda

I wanted to take just a moment to thank you for reading A Familiar Tail. I truly hope it gave you a little bit of pleasure in all the craziness that is the world right now.

Please check out my website at BelindaWrites.com for updates on upcoming books. I'll try to keep it updated, but fair warning: I'm really bad at that sort of thing. I promise I'll try to do better.

Also, if you can spare a few minutes, please consider giving my book a review. I'd really appreciate knowing what you thought of it.

There are lots more Gemstone Coven novels to come! Look for Opal's series to start in the next few months. I'm having a lot of fun with it!

Belinda White
March 2020